Paddington
Here and Now

Michael Bond

Paddington
Here and Now

Illustrated by
Peggy Fortnum

HarperCollins *Children's Books*

First published in hardback in Great Britain by HarperCollins Children's Books in 2008
First published in paperback in 2009
This edition published in 2014

2

HarperCollins Children's Books is a division of HarperCollins*Publishers* Ltd,
77-85 Fulham Palace Road, Hammersmith, London W6 8JB.

Visit our website at:
www.harpercollins.co.uk

Cover illustrations adapted and coloured by Mark Burgess
from the originals by Peggy Fortnum

ISBN: 978-0-00-794357-9

Originated by Dot Gradations Ltd, UK
Printed in Great Britain by
Clays Ltd, St Ives plc

MIX
Paper from
responsible sources
FSC
www.fsc.org
FSC® C007454

CONTENTS

Chapter One

PARKING PROBLEMS

"MY SHOPPING BASKET on wheels has been towed away!" exclaimed Paddington hotly.

He gazed at the spot where he had left it before going into the cut-price grocers in the Portobello Market. In all the years he had lived in London such a thing had never happened to him before and he could hardly believe his eyes. But if he thought staring at the empty space was going to make it reappear he was doomed to disappointment.

"It's coming to something if a young bear gent can't leave 'is shopping basket unattended for five minutes while 'e's going about 'is business," said one of the stallholders, who normally supplied Paddington with vegetables when he was out shopping for the Brown family. "I don't know what the world's coming to."

"There's no give and take any more," agreed a man at the next stall. "It's all take and no give. They'll be towing *us* away next, you mark my words."

"You should have left a note on it saying 'Back in five minutes'," said a third one.

"Fat lot of good that would have done," said another. "They don't give you five seconds these days, let alone five minutes."

Paddington was a popular figure in the market and by now a small crowd of sympathisers had begun to gather. Although he was known to drive a hard bargain, he was much respected by the traders. Receiving his custom was regarded by many as being something of an honour: on a par with having a sign saying they were by appointment to a member of the Royal Family.

"The foreman of the truck said it was in the way of his vehicle," said a lady who had witnessed the event. "They were trying to get behind a car they wanted to tow away."

"But my buns were in it," said Paddington.

"*Were*, is probably the right word," replied the lady. "I dare say even now they're parked in some side street or other wolfing them down. Driving those great big tow-away trucks of theirs must give them an appetite."

"I don't know what Mr Gruber is going to say when he hears," said Paddington. "They were meant for our elevenses."

"Look on the bright side," said another lady. "At least you've still got your suitcase with you. The basket could have been clamped. That would have cost you £80 to get it undone."

"And you would have to hang about half the day before they got around to doing it," agreed another.

Paddington's face grew longer and longer as he listened to all the words of wisdom. "Eighty pounds!" he exclaimed. "But I only went in for Mrs Bird's bottled water!"

"You can buy a new basket on wheels in the market for £10," chimed in another stallholder.

"I dare say if you haggle a bit you could get one for a lot less," said another.

"But I've only got ten pence," said Paddington sadly. "Besides, I wouldn't want a new one. Mr Brown gave mine to me soon after I arrived. I've had it ever since."

"Quite right!" agreed an onlooker. "You stick to your guns. They don't come like that these days. Them new ones is all plastic. Don't last five minutes."

"If you ask me," said a lady who ran a knick-knacks stall, "it's a pity it *didn't* get clamped. My Sid would have lent you his hacksaw like a shot. He doesn't hold with that kind of thing."

"Pity you weren't here in person when they did it," said another stallholder. "You would have been able to lie down in the road in front of their truck as a protest. Then we could have phoned the local press to send over one of their photographers and it would have been in all the papers."

"That would have stopped the lorry in its tracks," agreed someone else from the back of the crowd.

Paddington eyed the man doubtfully. "Supposing it didn't?" he said.

"In that case you would have been on the

evening news," said the man. "Television would have had a field day interviewing all the witnesses."

"You'd have become what they call a martyr," agreed the first man. "I dare say in years to come they would have erected a statue in your honour. Then nobody would have been able to park."

"What you need," said the fruit and vegetable man, summing up the whole situation, "is a good lawyer. Someone like Sir Bernard Crumble. He lives just up the road. This kind of thing is just up his street. He's a great one for sticking up for the underdog…" he broke off as he caught Paddington's eye. "Well, I dare say he does under*bears* as well. He'd have their guts for garters. Never been known to lose a case yet."

"Which street does he live in?" asked Paddington hopefully.

"I shouldn't get ideas above your station," warned another trader. "If you'll pardon the pun. They do say 'e charges an arm and a leg just to open 'is front door to the postman."

"If I were you," said a passer-by, "before you do anything else, I suggest you go along to the police station and report the matter to them. I dare say they'll be able to arrange counselling for you."

"Whatever you do," advised one of the stallholders, "don't tell them you've been towed away. Be what they call non committal. Just say your vehicle has gone missing."

He gazed at the large pack of bottled water Paddington had bought in the grocers. "You can leave those with me. I'll make sure they don't come to any harm."

Paddington thanked the man for his kind offer and after waving goodbye to the crowd he set off at a brisk pace towards the nearest police station.

But as he turned a corner and a familiar blue lamp came into view, he began to slow down. Over the years he had met a number of policemen and he had always found them only too ready to help in times of trouble. There was the occasion when he'd mistaken a television repairman for a burglar, and another time when he had bought some oil shares from a man in the market and they had turned out to be dud.

But he had never actually gone into a police station all by himself before, and not knowing what to expect he began to wish he had consulted his friend, Mr Gruber, before taking the plunge. Mr Gruber was always ready to help, and he most certainly would have done so had he heard their buns were missing. He might even have closed his shop for the morning.

And if he couldn't do that for any reason, there was always Mrs Bird. Mrs Bird looked after the Browns, and she didn't stand for any nonsense, especially if she thought Paddington was being hard done by.

However, as things turned out, he was pleasantly surprised when he mounted the steps and pushed the door slightly ajar. Apart from a man in uniform behind a counter, the room was completely empty.

The man was much younger than he had expected. In fact, he didn't seem much older than Mr and Mrs Brown's son, Jonathan, who was still at school. He looked slightly apprehensive when he caught sight of Paddington, rather as though he didn't know quite what to make of him.

"Er... *Sprechen Sie Deutsch*?" he ventured nervously.

"Bless you," said Paddington, politely raising his hat. "You can borrow my handkerchief if you like."

The policeman gave him a funny look before trying again.

"*Parlez-vous français?*"

"Not today, thank you," said Paddington.

"Pardon me for asking," said the officer. "But it's 'Be Polite to Foreigners Week'. Strictly unofficial, of course. It's the Sergeant's idea because we get a lot of overseas visitors at this time of the year, especially round the Portobello Road area, and I thought perhaps…"

"I'm not a foreigner," exclaimed Paddington hotly. "I'm from Darkest Peru."

The policeman looked put out. "Well, if that doesn't make you a foreigner, I don't know what does," he said. "Mind you, it takes all sorts. I must say you speak very good English, wherever you're from."

"My Aunt Lucy taught me before she went into the Home for Retired Bears in Lima," said Paddington.

"Well, she did a good job, I'll say that for her," said the policeman. "What can we do for you?"

"I've come to see you about my vehicle," said Paddington, choosing his words with care. "It isn't where I left it."

"And where was that?" asked the policeman.

"Outside the cut-price grocers in the market," said Paddington. "I always leave it there when I'm out shopping."

"Oh, dear," said the officer. "Not another one gone missing. There's a lot of it about at the moment, especially round these parts…" He reached for a computer keyboard. "I'd better take down some details."

"It had my buns in it," said Paddington.

"That's not a lot to go on," said the policeman. "I was wondering what make it is?"

"It's not really a make," said Paddington vaguely. "Mr Brown built it for me when I first went to stay with them."

"Home-made," said the officer, typing in the words. "Ahhhhh! Colour?"

"I think it's called wickerwork," said Paddington.

"I'll put down yellow for the time being," said the man. "Did you leave the handbrake on? That always slows them down a bit when they want to make a quick getaway."

"It doesn't have a handbrake," said Paddington. "It doesn't even have a paw brake. If I need to stop on a hill I usually put some stones under the wheels. Especially if I've been to get the potatoes."

"Potatoes?" echoed the policeman. "What have potatoes got to do with it?"

"They weigh a lot," explained Paddington. "Especially King Edwards. If my vehicle started to roll down a hill I don't know what I would do. I expect I would close my eyes in case it hit something and all the potatoes fell out."

The policeman looked up from his keyboard and stared at Paddington. "I'll pretend I didn't hear that," he said, not unkindly. "That sort of thing wouldn't go down too well if it was read out in court. You might find yourself ending up in prison.

"Mind you," he continued. "It's probably on its way to the Czech Republic or somewhere like that by now."

"The Czech Republic!" exclaimed Paddington hotly. "But it's only just gone ten o'clock."

"You'd be surprised," said the man. "These people don't lose any time. A quick going over with a spray gun. Who knows what colour it is by now. A new numberplate... On the other hand we don't let the grass grow under our feet." He picked up a telephone. "I'll put out an all stations call."

"I don't have one of those," said Paddington, looking most relieved.

"One of what?" asked the policeman, holding his hand over the mouthpiece.

"A numberplate," said Paddington.

The policeman replaced the receiver. "Hold on a minute," he said. "You'll be telling me next you haven't renewed your road tax…"

"I haven't," said Paddington. He stared back at the man with growing excitement. It really was uncanny the way he knew about all the things he hadn't got.

"I'm glad I came here," he said. "I didn't know you had to pay taxes."

"Ignorance of the law is no excuse," said the policeman sternly. Reaching under the counter he produced a large card showing a selection of pictures.

"I take it you are conversant with road signs?"

Paddington peered at the card. "We didn't have anything like that in Darkest Peru," he said. "But there's one near where I live."

The policeman pointed at random to one of the

pictures. "What does that one show?"

"A man trying to open an umbrella," said Paddington promptly. "I expect it means it's about to rain."

"It's meant to depict a man with a shovel," said the policeman wearily. "That means there are roadworks ahead. If you ask me, you need to read your Highway Code again. Unless, of course…"

"You're quite right," broke in Paddington, more than ever pleased he had come to the police station. "I've never read it."

"I think it's high time I saw your driving licence," said the policeman.

"I haven't got one of those either," exclaimed Paddington excitedly.

"Insurance?"

"What's that?" asked Paddington.

"What's that?" repeated the policeman. "*What's that*?"

He ran his fingers round the inside of his collar. The room had suddenly become very hot. "You'll be telling me next," he said, "that you haven't even passed your driving test."

"You're quite right," said Paddington excitedly. "I took it once by mistake, but I didn't pass because I drove into the examiner's car. I was in Mr Brown's car at the time and I had it in reverse by mistake. I don't think he was very pleased."

"Examiners are funny that way," said the policeman. "Bears like you are a menace to other road users."

"Oh, I never go on the road," said Paddington. "Not unless I have to. I always stick to the path."

The policeman gave him a long, hard look. He seemed to have grown older in the short time Paddington had been there. "You do realise," he said, "that I could throw the book at you."

"I hope you don't," said Paddington earnestly. "I'm not very good at catching things. It isn't easy with paws."

The policeman looked nervously over his shoulder before reaching into his back pocket.

"Talking of paws," he said casually, as he came round to the front of the counter. "Would you mind holding yours out in front of you?"

Paddington did as he was bidden, and to his

surprise there was a click and he suddenly found his wrists held together by some kind of chain.

"I hope you have a good lawyer," said the policeman. "You're going to need one. You won't have a leg to stand on otherwise."

"I shan't have a leg to stand on?" repeated Paddington in alarm. He gave the man a hard stare. "But I had two when I came in!"

"I'm going to take your dabs now," said the policeman.

"My *dabs*!" repeated Paddington in alarm.

"Fingerprints," explained the policeman. "Only in your case I suppose we shall have to make do with paws. First of all I want you to press one of them down on this ink pad, then on some paper, so that we have a record of it for future reference."

"Mrs Bird won't be very pleased if it comes off on the sheets," said Paddington.

"After that," said the policeman, ignoring the interruption, "you are allowed one telephone call."

"In that case," said Paddington, "I would like to ring Sir Bernard Crumble. He lives near here. He's supposed to be very good on motoring offences. I don't know if he does shopping baskets on wheels, but if he does, they told me in the market that he will have your guts for garters."

The policeman stared at him. "Did I hear you say shopping basket on wheels?" he exclaimed. "Why ever didn't you tell me that in the first place?"

"You didn't ask me," said Paddington. "I have a special licence for it. It was given to me when I failed my driving test in a car. They said it would last me all my life. I expect Sir Bernard will want to see it. I keep it in a secret compartment of my suitcase. I can show it to you if you like. At least, I could if I had it with me and I was able to use my paws."

He stared at the policeman, who seemed to have gone a pale shade of white. "Is anything the matter?" he asked. "Would you like a marmalade sandwich? I keep one under my hat in case of an emergency."

The policeman shook his head. "No, thank you," he groaned, as he removed the handcuffs. "It's my first week on duty. They told me I might have some difficult customers to deal with, but I didn't think it would start quite so soon…"

"I can come back later if you like," said Paddington hopefully.

"I'd much rather you didn't…" began the policeman. He broke off as a door opened and an older man came into the room. He had some stripes on his sleeve and he looked very important.

"Ah," said the man, consulting a piece of paper he was holding. "Bush hat… blue duffle coat… Fits the description I was given over the phone… You must be the young gentleman who's had trouble with his shopping basket on wheels."

He turned to the first policeman. "You did well to keep him talking, Finsbury. Full marks."

"It was nothing, Sarge," said the constable, who seemed to have got some of his colour back.

"It seems there's been a bit of a mix-up with the lads in the tow-away department," continued the sergeant, turning back to Paddington. "They put your basket on their vehicle for safe keeping while they were removing a car and forgot to take it off again. It went back to the depot with them.

"They've put some fresh buns in it for you. Apparently, somehow or other, the ones that were in it got lost *en route*. Even now, the basket's on its way back to where you left it. And there's nothing to pay. What do you say to that?"

"Thank you very much, Mr Sarge," said Paddington gratefully. "It means I shan't have to speak to Sir Bernard Crumble after all. If you don't mind, I shall always come here first if ever my shopping basket on wheels gets towed away."

"That's what we're here for," said the sergeant. "Although I think I should warn you; it may be a bit heavier now than when you first set out this morning."

"Quite right too," said Paddington's friend, Mr Gruber, when they eventually sat down to their elevenses and Paddington told him the full story, including the moment when he got back to the market and found to his surprise that his basket on wheels was full to the top with fruit and vegetables.

"You have been a very good customer over the years and I dare say none of the traders want to see you go elsewhere. It is a great compliment to you, Mr Brown.

"All the same," he continued, "it must have been a nasty experience while it lasted. If I were you, I would start your elevenses before the cocoa gets cold. You must be in need of it."

Paddington thought that was a very good idea indeed. "Perhaps," he said, looking up at the antique clock on the wall of the shop, "just this once, Mr Gruber, we ought to call it 'twelveses'."

Chapter Two

PADDINGTON'S GOOD TURN

LIKE MOST HOUSEHOLDS up and down the country, number thirty-two Windsor Gardens had its own set routine.

In the case of the Brown family, Mr Brown usually went off to his office soon after breakfast, leaving Mrs Brown and Mrs Bird to go about their daily tasks. Most days, apart from the times when

Jonathan and Judy were home for the school holidays, Paddington spent the morning visiting his friend, Mr Gruber, for cocoa and buns.

There were occasional upsets, of course, but on the whole the household was like an ocean liner. It steamed happily on its way, no matter what the weather.

So when Mrs Bird returned home one day to what she fully expected to be an empty house and saw a strange face peering at her through the landing window, it took a moment or two to recover from the shock, and by then whoever it was had gone.

What made it far worse, was the fact that she was halfway up the stairs to her bedroom at the time, which meant the face belonged to someone *outside* the house.

She hadn't seen any sign of a ladder on her way in; but all the same she rushed back downstairs again, grabbed the first weapon she could lay her hands on, and dashed out into the garden.

Apart from a passing cat, which gave a loud shriek and scuttled off with its tail between its legs when it caught sight of her umbrella, everything appeared to be normal, so it was a mystery and no mistake.

When they heard the news later that day, Mr and Mrs Brown couldn't help wondering if Mrs Bird had been mistaken, but they didn't say so to her face in case she took umbrage.

"Perhaps it was a window cleaner gone to the wrong house," suggested Mr Brown.

"In that case he made a very quick getaway," said Mrs Bird. "I wouldn't fancy having him do our windows."

"I suppose it could have been a trick of the light," said Mrs Brown.

Mrs Bird gave one of her snorts.

"I know what I saw," she said darkly. "And whatever it was, or *who*ever it was, they were up to no good."

The Browns knew better than to argue, and Paddington, who had been given a detective outfit for his birthday, spent some time testing the windowsill for clues. Much to his disappointment he couldn't find any marks on it other than his own. All the same, he took some measurements and carefully wrote the details down in his notebook.

In an effort to restore calm, Mr Brown rang the police, but they were unable to be of much help either.

"It sounds to me like the work of 'Gentleman Dan, the Drainpipe Man'," said the officer who came to visit them. "They do say he's usually in the Bahamas at this time of the year, but he could be back earlier than usual if the weather's bad.

"He didn't get his name for nothing. He bides his time until he sees what he thinks are some empty premises, and then he shins up the nearest drainpipe. He can be in and out of a house like a flash of lightning. Never leaves any trace of what we in the force call 'his dabs', on account of the fact that being a perfect gentleman he always wears gloves."

The Browns felt they had done all they could to allay Mrs Bird's fears, but the officer left them with one final piece of advice.

"We shall be keeping a lookout in the area for the next few days," he said, "in case he strikes again. But if I were you, to be on the safe side, I'd invest in a can of Miracle non-dry, anti-burglar paint and give your downpipes a coat as soon as possible.

"It's available at all good do-it-yourself shops. Mark my words, you won't be troubled again, and if by any chance you are, the perpetrator will be so covered in black paint, he won't get very far before we pick him up.

"Not only that," he said, addressing Mr Brown before driving off in his squad car, "you may find you get a reduction on your insurance policy."

"It sounds as though he's got shares in the company," said Mr Brown sceptically, as he followed his wife back indoors. "Either that or he has a spare-time job as one of their salesmen."

"Henry!" exclaimed Mrs Brown.

In truth, the next day was a Friday, and after a busy week at the office Mr Brown had been looking forward to a quiet weekend. The thought of spending it up a ladder painting drainpipes was not high on his list of priorities.

In normal circumstances he might not have taken up Paddington's offer to help quite so readily.

"Are you sure it's wise?" asked Mrs Brown, when he told her. "It's all very well Paddington saying bears are good at painting, but he says that about a lot of things. Remember what happened when he decorated the spare room."

"That was years ago," said Mr Brown. "Anyway, the fact that he ended up wallpapering over the door and couldn't find his way out again had nothing to do with the actual painting. Besides, it's not as if it's something we shall be looking at all the time. Even Paddington can't do much harm painting a drainpipe."

"I wouldn't be so sure," warned Mrs Bird. "Besides, it isn't just one drainpipe. There are at least half a dozen dotted round the house. And don't forget, it's non-dry paint. If that bear makes any mistakes, the marks will be there for ever more."

"There must come a time when it dries off," said Mr Brown optimistically.

"We could get Mr Briggs in," suggested Mrs Brown, mentioning their local decorator. "He's always ready to oblige."

But Mr Brown's mind was made up, and when he arrived back from his office that evening he brought with him a large can of paint and an assortment of brushes.

Paddington was very excited when he saw them, and he couldn't wait to get started.

That night, he took the can of paint up to bed and read the small print on the side with the aid of a torch and the magnifying glass from his detective outfit.

According to the instructions, a lot of burglars climbed drainpipes in order to break into people's homes. In fact, the more he read, the more Paddington began to wonder why he had never seen one before; it sounded as though the streets must be full of them. There was even a picture of one on the back of the tin. He looked very pleased with himself as he slid down a pipe, a sack over his shoulder bulging with things he had taken. There was even a 'thinks balloon' attached to his head saying: 'Don't you wish you had done something about *your* pipes?'

Paddington opened his bedroom window and peered outside, but luckily there were no drainpipes anywhere near it, otherwise he might have tested the paint there and then, just to be on the safe side.

Before going to sleep he made out a list of all the other requirements ready for the morning. Something with which to open the tin; a wire brush for cleaning the pipes before starting work; a pair of folding steps – the instructions suggested it was only necessary to paint the bottom half of the pipe, there was no need to go all the way up to the top; and some white spirit to clean the brushes afterwards.

The following morning, as soon as breakfast was over, he waylaid Mrs Bird in the kitchen and persuaded her to let him have some plastic gloves and an old apron.

Knowing who would be landed with the task of getting any paint stains off his duffle coat if things went wrong, the Browns' housekeeper was only too willing to oblige.

"Mind you don't get any of that stuff on your whiskers," she warned, as he disappeared out of the back door armed with his list. "You don't want to spoil your elevenses."

Paddington's suggestion that it might be a good idea to have them *before* he started work fell on deaf ears, so he set to work gathering the things he needed from the garage. While he was there he came across a special face mask to keep out paint fumes.

Clearly, it wasn't meant for bears, because although it covered the end of his nose, it was nowhere near his eyes. All the same, having slipped the elastic bands over his ears to hold it in place, he spent some time looking at his reflection in the wing mirror of Mr Brown's car and as far as he could make out all his whiskers were safely tucked away inside it.

Once in the garden he set to work with a wire brush on a rainwater pipe at the rear of the house.

"I must say he looks like some creature from outer space," said Mrs Bird, gazing out of the kitchen window.

"At least it keeps him occupied," said Mrs Brown. "I can't help being uneasy whenever he's at a loose end."

"The devil finds work for idle paws," agreed Mrs Bird, almost immediately wishing she hadn't said it in case she was tempting fate.

But much to everyone's surprise Paddington made such a good job of the first pipes,

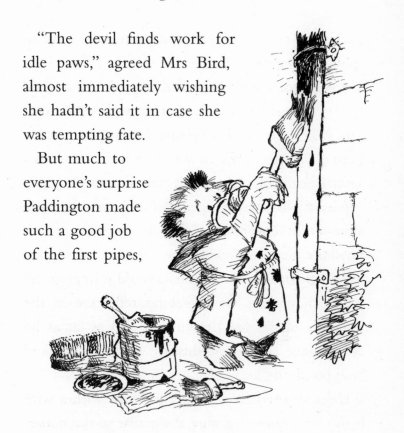

even Mrs Bird's eagle eyes couldn't find anything amiss when she inspected them. There wasn't a single spot of paint to be seen anywhere on the surrounding brickwork.

And even if it meant she would never be able to use her plastic gloves or her apron again, she didn't have the heart to complain. It was a small price to pay for having number thirty-two Windsor Gardens made secure, *and* keeping Paddington occupied into the bargain.

"What did I tell you, Mary?" said Mr Brown, looking up from his morning paper when she passed on the news.

"I only hope he doesn't try shinning up the pipes to see if it works," said Mrs Brown. "You know how keen he is on testing things."

"It's a bit like giving someone a hot plate and telling them not to touch it," agreed Mrs Bird.

As it happened, similar thoughts had been going through Paddington's mind most of the morning. At one point when he stopped for a rest he even toyed with the idea of hiding round a corner in the hope that Gentleman Dan might turn up, but with only one more drainpipe to go he decided he'd better finish off the work as quickly as possible.

It was the one just outside the landing window at the side of the house, which had been the cause of all the trouble in the first place, and he had left it until last because he wanted to make an especially good job of it for Mrs Bird's sake.

Having scrubbed the bottom section of the pipe clean with the wire brush, he mounted the steps and began work on the actual painting.

He hadn't been doing it for very long before he heard a familiar voice.

"What are you doing, bear?" barked Mr Curry.

Paddington nearly fell off the steps with alarm. The last person he wanted to see was the Browns' next-door neighbour.

"I'm painting Mr Brown's drainpipes," he announced, regaining his balance.

"I can see that," growled Mr Curry suspiciously. "The thing is, bear, why are you doing it?"

"It's some special paint which never dries," said Paddington. "It's very good value."

"Paint which never dries?" repeated the Browns' neighbour. "It doesn't sound very good value to me."

"It was recommended to Mr Brown by a

policeman," said Paddington importantly. "I've nearly finished all the pipes and I haven't used half the tin yet.

"Mrs Bird saw a face at the window when she came home from her shopping the other day," he explained, seeing the sceptical look on Mr Curry's face.

"The policeman thought it might have been someone called 'Gentleman Dan, the Drainpipe Man' who climbed up this very pipe. Mrs Bird said it gave her quite a turn. She hasn't got over it yet."

"I'm not surprised," said Mr Curry. "Let's hope they catch him."

"I don't think he'll be back," said Paddington. "Not if he saw Mrs Bird on the warpath, but Mr Brown thinks it's better to be safe than sorry."

"Hmm," said Mr Curry. "What did you say it's called, bear?"

"Miracle non-dry paint for outside use," said Paddington, reading from the can. He held it up for Mr Curry to see. "You can buy it at any good do-it-yourself shop."

"I don't want to do-it-myself, bear!" growled Mr Curry. "I have more important things to do.

Besides, I'm on my way out."

He paused for a moment. "On the other hand, I would be more than interested in having my own pipes done. I do have some very valuable items about the house. Family heirlooms, you know."

"Have you really?" said Paddington with interest. "I don't think I've ever seen an heirloom before."

"And you're not starting with mine," said the Browns' neighbour shortly.

"I don't have them on display for every Tom, Dick and bear to see. I keep them tucked away – out of the sight of prying eyes."

Paddington couldn't help thinking if that were the case there was no point in the Browns' neighbour having his drainpipes painted, but Mr Curry was notorious for being unable to resist getting something for nothing, even if it was something he didn't need.

A cunning look came over his face. "Did you say you have over half a tin of paint left?" he asked.

"Nearly," said Paddington. He was beginning to wish he hadn't mentioned it in the first place.

Mr Curry felt in his trouser pocket. "Perhaps you

would like to have a go at my pipes while you're at it," he said. "I'm afraid I don't have very much change on me, but I could stretch to ten pence if you do a good job."

Paddington did a quick count-up on his paws. "Ten pence!" he exclaimed. "That's less than tuppence a pipe!"

"It's a well-known fact in business," said Mr Curry, "that the bigger the quantity, the less you pay for each individual item. It's what's known as giving discount."

"In that case," said Paddington hopefully, "perhaps I could do one of your pipes for five pence?"

"Ten pence for the lot," said Mr Curry firmly. "That's my final offer. There's no point in having only one done."

"I think I'd better ask Mr Brown if he minds first," said Paddington, clutching at straws. "It is his paint."

"Now you don't want to do that, bear," said Mr Curry, hastily changing his tune. "Let it be between ourselves."

Reaching into his pocket again, he lowered his

voice. "As I say, I have to go out now and I probably won't be back until this evening, so that will give you plenty of time to get it done. But, if you make a really good job of it, I may give you a little extra. Here's something to be going on with."

Before Paddington had a chance to answer, something landed with a 'plop' on the gravel at the foot of his steps.

Climbing down, he picked up the object and gazed at it for a moment or two before glancing up at Mr Curry's house. Unlike the Browns' drainpipes, they looked as though they hadn't seen a paintbrush in  years. His heart sank as he turned the coin over in his paw. For a start it didn't even look English. In fact, the more he thought about it the less exciting Mr Curry's offer seemed, particularly when it meant doing something he hadn't bargained on in the first place.

While Paddington was considering the matter, he heard Mr Curry's front door slam shut. It was followed almost immediately afterwards by a clang from the front gate, and that, in turn, triggered off one of his brainwaves.

Shortly afterwards Paddington was hard at work again, and this time, knowing how cross the Browns would be on his behalf were they able to see what he was doing, he intended getting it over and done with as quickly as possible.

Later that day the Browns were in the middle of their afternoon tea when the peace was shattered by the sound of a violent commotion in the road outside their house.

At one point Mrs Bird thought she heard loud cries of "Bear", and shortly afterwards there was the sound of a police siren, but by the time she got to the front window all was quiet.

They had hardly settled down again before there was a ring at the front door bell.

"I'll go this time, Mrs Bird!" said Paddington eagerly, and before the others could stop him he was on his way.

When he returned, he was accompanied by the policeman who had visited them earlier in the week.

"Will someone please tell me what's going on?" said Mr Brown.

"Allow me," said the officer before Paddington had a chance to open his mouth.

He produced his notebook. "First of all, a short while ago we received a call from one of your neighbours reporting a disturbance outside number thirty-three. We arrived at the scene as quickly as we could. The gate was wide open and a gentleman covered in black paint was dancing about in the gutter, shouting his head off. Assuming it must be Gentleman Dan, the Drainpipe Man, we placed him under immediate arrest.

"On our way back to the station, we managed to quieten him down..." the policeman looked up from his notebook, "which was no easy task, I can tell you. He informed us he was your next-door neighbour, so we removed the handcuffs and brought him back. I dare say you will be able to confirm you have a Mr Curry living next door."

"I'm afraid we do," said Mrs Brown.

"What did he look like?" asked Mr Brown.

"Well, he's not exactly a bear lover for a start," said the policeman. "Kept going on about the iniquities of someone called Paddington…"

"Say no more," broke in Mrs Bird. "That's him."

"Well," continued the officer, "when we arrived back at his house, who should we meet coming out of the gate, but none other than Gentleman Dan, the Drainpipe Man. He must have seen us drive off and seized his chance.

"He had the cheek to say he'd gone to the wrong door by mistake."

"Did he get away with much?" asked Mr Brown.

"Didn't have a thing on him," said the officer, "which is a pity, because I gather from Mr Curry that he has a lot of valuable items, and we could have booked him on the spot.

"On the other hand, I don't think he'll be bothering us again for a while. Thanks to this young bear's efforts, we've not only got a picture of him, but we have his 'dabs' for good measure."

He turned to Paddington. "I'd like to shake you

by the paw for your sterling work," he said.

Paddington eyed the policeman's hand doubtfully. There was a large lump of something black attached to the palm.

"Perhaps you would like to borrow some of Mr Brown's white spirit first," he said. "You won't want to get any of that on your steering wheel."

"You've got a point," said the policeman, taking a look at it himself. "Seeing as how I recommended it in the first place, I can't really complain, but…"

"I still don't quite understand," said Mr Brown, after the officer had left. "What's all this about painting Mr Curry's front gate?"

Paddington took a deep breath. "I thought if I stopped any burglars getting into his garden in the first place, they wouldn't be able to break into his house, and it would save using up all your paint on his downpipes. I forgot Mr Curry still had to get back in!"

The Browns fell silent as they digested this latest piece of information.

"It seemed like a good idea at the time," said Paddington lamely.

"You can't really blame Paddington, Henry," said Mrs Brown. "You did take him up on his offer after all."

"How much was Mr Curry going to pay you for doing his pipes?" asked Mr Brown.

"Ten pence," said Paddington

"In that case," said Mrs Bird, amid general agreement, "I have no sympathy. That man deserves all he gets. *And* he knows it.

"If he says anything to you about it," she added grimly, turning to Paddington, "tell him to come and see me first."

"Thank you very much, Mrs Bird," said Paddington gratefully. "If you like, I'll go round and tell him now."

The Browns exchanged glances. "It's very kind of you, Paddington," said Mrs Brown. "But you've had a very busy day, and I do think it's a case of 'least said, soonest mended'. Why don't you put your paws up for a while?"

Having considered the matter, Paddington

thought it was a very good idea indeed. And funnily enough, Mr Curry never did mention the day he *didn't* get his drainpipes painted, although for some weeks to come, whenever Paddington waved to the Browns' neighbour over the garden fence he received some very black looks in return.

They were even darker than the colour of his front gate, which now remained permanently open.

On the other hand, Mrs Bird never again saw a face looking at her through the landing window.

Chapter Three

PADDINGTON STRIKES A CHORD

PADDINGTON ALWAYS LOOKED forward to his morning chats with Mr Gruber. One of the things that made visiting his friend's antique shop in the Portobello Road so special was the fact that it was never the same two days running. People came from far and wide to seek Mr Gruber's advice. If it wasn't someone looking for an old painting or a bronze statue, it was someone else browsing through his vast collection of books, which covered practically every subject under the sun.

In time, Paddington became quite knowledgeable about antiques himself; so much so, he could immediately tell a piece of genuine Spode china from an ordinary run-of-the-mill item of crockery, although he would never have dared pick any of it up in case he dropped it by mistake.

"Better safe than sorry," was Mr Gruber's motto.

That apart, since both of them had begun life in a foreign country, they were never short of things to talk about.

During the summer months they often had their elevenses sitting in deck chairs on the pavement outside the shop, discussing problems of the day in peace and quiet before the crowds arrived.

Paddington couldn't help but notice his friend usually had a faraway look in his eyes whenever he spoke of his native Hungary.

"When I was a boy," Mr Gruber would say, "people used to dance the night away to the sound of balalaikas. That doesn't seem to happen any more."

Having been born in Darkest Peru, Paddington had no idea what a balalaika was, let alone what it sounded like, but with Mr Gruber's help he did learn to play a tune called "Chopsticks" on an ancient piano at the back of the shop.

It wasn't easy, because having paws meant he often played several notes at the same time, but Mr Gruber said anyone with half an ear for music would recognise it at once.

"Music is a wonderful thing, Mr Brown," he was wont to say. "Chopsticks may not be top of what is known as 'the Pops', but if you are able to play it on the piano you will always be in demand at parties."

On cloudy days, when there was a chill in the air, they made a habit of retiring to an old horsehair sofa at the back of the shop, and it was on just such a morning, soon after his adventure with the shopping basket on wheels, that Paddington arrived rather earlier than usual and found to his surprise that Mr Gruber had acquired a new piano.

It was standing in almost exactly the same spot as the old one had been; near the stove where his friend made the cocoa.

There was no sign of Mr Gruber, which was most unusual, so to pass the time Paddington decided to have a go at playing what had become known as 'his tune', when something very strange happened.

As he raised his paws to play the opening notes, the keys began going up and down all by themselves!

He had hardly finished rubbing his eyes in order to make sure he wasn't dreaming, when he had yet another surprise. Out of the corner of his eye he saw Mr Gruber crawl out from underneath a nearby table.

"Oh dear," said Paddington, "I hope I haven't broken your new piano."

Mr Gruber laughed. "Have no fear of that, Mr Brown," he said. "It is what is known as a 'player piano' and it works by electricity. You don't see many around these days. I've just been plugging it in to make sure it works properly."

"I don't think I have ever seen a piano that plays a tune all by itself before," said Paddington. "We didn't have anything like that in Darkest Peru. But then we didn't have electricity either," he added sadly.

While Mr Gruber set about making the cocoa, Paddington took a closer look at the keyboard. It really was uncanny the way the keys went up and down in time to the music, and he tried following their movement with his paws without actually touching them. In the beginning he found it was hard to keep up with them, but after several goes it really began to look as though he was actually playing the tune.

"Look, Mr Gruber," he called. "I can even do it cross paws!"

"I should watch out," warned his friend, looking up from the saucepan. "It's the *Tritsch Tratsch Polka*. You will need to sit very tight."

But it was too late. Even as Mr Gruber spoke, the music reached a crescendo and Paddington suddenly found himself lying on the floor with his legs in the air.

Mr Gruber ran to switch the machine off. "I'm afraid it's a case of trying to run before you can walk, Mr Brown," he said, helping Paddington to his feet. "I think perhaps you should try starting with something a little slower. I will see what I can find."

Opening the lid of a long cardboard box, he produced a roll of paper on a spindle, and unwinding it slightly, he held it up for Paddington to see.

Although he didn't say so, Paddington felt disappointed. It looked rather as if the moths had been at it.

"It seems to have a lot of holes in it," he said.

"Well spotted," said Mr Gruber. "You have hit the nail on the head as usual, Mr Brown. That is the secret behind a player piano. It works by blowing air through those holes as they go past. When the roll goes through at the correct speed, every time a hole passes a nozzle the blast of air sets a lever in motion, and that in turn operates the correct note on the keyboard."

While he was talking, Mr Gruber opened a small door above in the front of the piano, rewound the roll of paper already in there, and replaced it with the new one.

"It sounds very complicated," said Paddington, dusting himself down.

"It is really no more complicated than you or I picking up a mug of cocoa and drinking it," said Mr Gruber. "When you think about it, that is also something of a miracle. I suggest we have our elevenses first, and then you can try out the tune I've just put in. It's Beethoven's *Moonlight Sonata*. I'm sure you will find it much easier."

It sounded a very good idea, and Paddington hastily unpacked the morning supply of buns.

After they had finished the last of them and drained their mugs of cocoa, he climbed back on to the stool. This time, because the music was so much slower, he was even better at following the movement of the keys, and several passers-by stopped outside the shop to watch.

"I wonder if Mr Beethoven did a Chopsticks roll?" he said. "I expect he would have been very good at playing that."

"I doubt it," said Mr Gruber. "He was a very

famous composer and he wouldn't have had the time. Besides, this machine wasn't invented until long after he died.

"If you close your eyes," he continued, "and sway gently with the music, I'm sure a great many people will think you really are playing it."

Following his friend's instructions, Paddington had another go and by the time he reached the end of the piece, the pavement outside the shop was thronged with sightseers.

"Bravo!" said Mr Gruber, joining in the applause as Paddington stood up and bowed to the audience. "What did I tell you, Mr Brown? I think even Beethoven himself would have been taken in."

Shortly afterwards, having thanked Mr Gruber for the cocoa, Paddington bid him goodbye and made his way out of the shop, raising his hat to the crowd outside as he went. A number of people took his photograph, still more wanted his autograph, and several more dropped coins into his hat before he had a chance to put it back on. They felt quite cold when they landed on his head.

One way and another, he was so excited he couldn't wait to tell the Browns all about it, so as soon as he was able to escape from the crowd of admirers Paddington set off as fast as he could in the direction of Windsor Gardens.

He hadn't gone far before he realised he was being followed. In a strange way it wasn't unlike the player piano. Each time he put a foot down on the pavement, it was echoed by a footstep close behind him.

Looking back over his shoulder as he stopped at some traffic lights, he saw a figure wearing a long black overcoat and a fur hat waving at him.

"Stop! Stop!" called the man.

"This whole thing is quite extraordinary,"

continued the newcomer, removing a glove as he drew near. "I have never seen a bear play the piano before. Allow me to shake you by the, er… paw."

Paddington hastily wiped the nearest one on his duffle coat before holding it out.

"It's quite easy really," he began. "You see…"

"Ah, such modesty." The man glanced at Paddington's shopping basket on wheels. "I see you take your sheet music everywhere with you. How very wise."

"It isn't music," said Paddington. "It's Mrs Bird's vegetables."

Reaching inside the basket he took out a carrot and held it up for the other to see.

"Ah!" said the man, masking his disappointment. "It's good to see you haven't lost the common touch."

He pointed to a large poster on a nearby wall, one of many Paddington had recently seen dotted about the area. "I don't suppose for one moment you would care to do a recital for me, would you? I'm putting on a concert in aid of charity and a piano-playing bear is just the kind of thing I need to round things off. The icing on the cake as it were."

"Jonathan and Judy will be home for the half term and Mr Brown is taking us all to see it as a treat," said Paddington doubtfully. "So I shall be there anyway."

"Splendid!" exclaimed the man. "In fact, it couldn't be better."

"I shall have to ask Mr Gruber first," said Paddington. "It is his piano and he says there aren't many like it left in the world."

"Leave all that to me," said the man. "Don't say another word. You shall have the best piano that money can buy. One which will suit your unique talents. Your obbligatos have to be heard to be believed. As for your glissandos... words fail me."

Paddington had no idea what the man was talking about, but he couldn't help feeling pleased. "It isn't easy with paws," he admitted. "I fell off the stool when I was playing the *Trish Trash Polka.*"

"It happens to the best of players," said the man, brushing it aside. "Perhaps we had better have your paws insured. On the other hand, you may have been trying to run before you could walk."

Paddington stared at him. "It happened only this morning," he said excitedly. "And that's exactly what Mr Gruber said."

He considered the matter for a moment or two. "I shall need some rolls," he announced.

"My dear sir," the man raised his hands to high heaven. "You shall have all the rolls you need at the party afterwards. They will be yours for the asking."

"It will be too late then," said Paddington. "I need them while I'm playing."

"You do?" The man looked at him in amazement.

"This is fantastic," he cried. "A novelty act! I can hardly believe my ears. There may be other bears in the world who play the piano, although I can't say I've come across any before, but there can't be many who have their supper at the same time."

"If you like," said Paddington eagerly, "I could eat a marmalade sandwich while I'm playing. I usually keep one under my hat in case of an emergency."

The man went into ecstasies at the thought.

"I can see it all," he cried, closing his eyes as he gazed heavenwards. "You might save that until the end. It could bring the house down."

Paddington eyed him nervously. "I hope it doesn't land on me," he said.

"Ah, so you tell jokes as well," said the man. "This gets better and better."

Reaching into an inside pocket he produced

some papers. "May I have your signature, kind sir? I just happen to have a form in my pocket."

While he was talking he handed Paddington a gold pen. "Just sign along the dotted line."

Paddington did his best to oblige, and because the man looked important, he added his special paw print to show it was genuine.

"Forgive my asking," said the man, eyeing the print with interest. "Are you by any chance Russian?"

"I was," said Paddington, "but I'm nearly home now."

His words fell on deaf ears as the man tried reading the writing above the blobs. "Is that where you were born... Paddington?"

"No," said Paddington. "It's my name. I've always been called that, ever since Mr and Mrs Brown found me on the railway station."

"In that case, we must change it to avoid any confusion," said the man. "We don't want the audience turning up at the wrong place, do we?"

"Change it!" repeated Paddington hotly.

"How about Padoffski?" said the man. "It will

look better when I over-stamp the posters, but you're not to tell anyone that."

"How about Mrs Bird?" asked Paddington. "She doesn't like changes."

"Not until after the concert," said the man, tapping the side of his nose. "Let it be a surprise.

"Afterwards," he said, "we must strike while the iron's hot and look to the future. What would you say to a world tour?"

"I wouldn't mind visiting the Home for Retired Bears in Lima," said Paddington. "It would be a nice surprise for Aunt Lucy."

"I don't normally do retirement homes," said the man. "More often than not the audience is fast asleep by the end of the programme."

"I'm sure Aunt Lucy would poke them with her knitting needle if they were," said Paddington loyally.

"Mmm, yes." The man eyed him doubtfully. "We shall have to see. First things first. We need to think about your entrance on the night. It's a pity you can't come up through the floor, like cinema organs used to in the old days."

"I expect I could borrow Mr Brown's saw," said Paddington eagerly.

"I must say you're not short of ideas," said the man admiringly. "We shall make a very good team. Now that I am your manager I can see it all."

"You are?" exclaimed Paddington, looking most surprised.

"Remember," said the man, holding the piece of paper aloft. "You signed along the dotted line. It's all down here in black and white.

"Do you happen to know Purcell's *Passing By*?" he continued, before Paddington had a chance to reply.

"Is he really?" said Paddington, looking round. "I didn't see him."

"He is a famous composer," said the man. "And that's the name of a song he wrote. I thought I might include it in your programme."

"I'll ask Mr Gruber," said Paddington. "He's bound to know."

"I would rather you didn't," said the man. "In fact, I would much rather you didn't tell anyone."

He tapped the side of his nose again. "Mum's the word."

"How about Mrs Bird?" asked Paddington. "She's not a mum and she knows everything."

"Especially Mrs Bird by the sound of it," said the man. "Remember, walls have ears, and whatever else happens, we *must* keep it a secret until after the concert. Listen carefully and I will give you your instructions for the night."

"Wonders will never cease," said Mrs Bird, two mornings later. "Paddington's had a bath without being asked. He also wanted to know if I could get some stains off his duffle coat. He had a marmalade chunk stuck to one of the toggles."

"Oh, dear," said Mrs Brown. "That *is* a bit worrying."

Having a bear about the house was a heavy responsibility and there were times when it was hard to picture what was going on in Paddington's mind.

"He's been acting strangely these last two days," she said. "Ever since he got back from the market. He was going round peering at the walls this morning, and when I asked him if anything was the matter all he said was 'Mum's the word'. Then he began tapping the side of his nose."

"I shouldn't worry too much," said Mrs Bird. "There are no flies on that bear."

"I suppose that's why," said Mrs Brown vaguely.

"I only hope he enjoys the concert tonight," said the Browns' housekeeper.

"Paddington enjoys anything new," said Mrs Brown, trying to keep a brave face. "That's one of the nice things about him. Henry thought it would be a treat."

It crossed Mrs Bird's mind that since Mr Brown went off to work every morning he didn't have to face the consequences, but wisely, she kept her thoughts to herself.

"We shall have to wait and see," she said.

In the event, however, even Mrs Bird could hardly fault Paddington's behaviour during the first half of the evening's performance. He even insisted on being at the end of the row when they took their seats.

"I expect he wants to be near the ice creams," whispered Jonathan.

Much to the Browns' relief, it didn't look as if the show involved any audience participation. It only needed a mind-reader to ask for volunteers to go up on stage, or a magician who wanted to saw a member of the audience in two, and Paddington was usually the first to offer his services; almost always with disastrous results.

He didn't even embarrass them by eating one of his marmalade sandwiches during the interval.

"I'm saving it until later," he announced rather mysteriously.

The Browns heaved a sigh of relief. They still had vivid memories of the first time he had been taken to see a play. They had been occupying a box at the side of the stalls, and Paddington had been so excited he accidentally dropped one of his sandwiches on to the head of a man sitting in a seat below them. At least they were safe from anything like that happening.

It wasn't until the show was nearing the end that Mr Brown happened to glance along the row and realised Paddington was missing.

"Where can he have got to?" asked Mrs Brown anxiously. "We shall never hear the last of it if he misses the Grand Finale. It's supposed to be something spectacular."

"Miss it, nothing!" exclaimed Jonathan, who had

been sitting next to him. He pointed towards the stage as the curtain began to rise. "Look! He's in it!"

"Mercy me!" cried Mrs Bird as she caught sight of a grand piano with a familiar figure seated at the keyboard. "Whatever is that bear up to now?"

Sporadic applause greeted the surprise item, particularly as it was some while before anything actually happened. Having spent some time staring at an area above the keys with a hopeful expression on his face, almost as though he expected to see a door of some kind, Paddington climbed off the stool and went round to the side of the piano.

Raising the lid as best he could, he peered inside. But if he was hoping to find what he was looking for, he was clearly disappointed. After several loud twangs as he felt around with his paw, he closed the lid and disappeared underneath the piano.

Growing increasingly restive at the delay, certain sections of the audience began to boo, and there were one or two catcalls from rougher elements at the back of the hall.

When Paddington finally emerged he was mopping his brow, and there was a hunted look on his face as he called out to someone at the side of the stage.

"What did he say?" asked Mrs Bird.

"Something about not being able to find a socket," said Jonathan.

"Chopsticks, Mr Brown!" came a loud voice from somewhere nearby. "Chopsticks!"

"Hear! Hear!" shouted someone else, or it could have been the same person disguising his voice.

Gradually, the call was taken up by others until it seemed as though everyone was stamping their feet and shouting "Chopsticks" at the top of their voices.

As Paddington obliged, someone – it might have been the person who called out in the first place – led the audience in clapping to the beat of the music, and towards the end, when he produced a sandwich from under his hat and took a large nibble, cheers shook the rafters.

The applause as Paddington stood to take his bow was deafening. So much so, he began looking anxiously at the ceiling.

"Best turn I've seen in years," remarked a neighbour of the Browns as they left the theatre. "We shall be seeing that bear's name in lights one of these days."

"If you want my advice," said Mr Gruber with a twinkle in his eye, when he bumped into them further along the road, "I should retire at your peak, Mr Brown. Otherwise, you may find the going downhill from now on."

Paddington stared at his friend. It really was uncanny how things kept repeating themselves.

"That's exactly what my manager said!" he exclaimed. "But he did tell me he's earmarked some of the money for the Home for Retired Bears in Lima. I must send Aunt Lucy a postcard and tell her to expect it."

Jonathan gave his sister a nudge. "I didn't know he had a manager. I wonder if that's who it was calling out for Chopsticks?"

"He certainly saved the day," said Judy. "Have you any idea who it was, Mr Gruber?"

But for some reason best known to himself, Paddington's friend was making haste to wave goodnight.

"To sum up," said Mrs Bird, as they turned into Windsor Gardens and the familiar green front door of number thirty-two came into view, "it proves there's a lot of truth in the old saying 'A friend in need is a friend indeed.'"

Chapter Four

PADDINGTON TAKES THE BISCUIT

ONE MORNING THE Brown family was about to sit down to breakfast as usual, when Mr Brown noticed something strange going on in the garden.

"What *is* Paddington up to?" he said, as a familiar figure in a duffle coat dashed past the French windows. "That's my best broom he's got hold of."

"Perhaps he's sweeping up," said Jonathan. "It

looks as though he's got a book of instructions."

"Even Paddington can't need instructions to sweep the patio," said Mr Brown.

"Besides, it's my lawn broom. It's a special one made of twigs."

"Quick!" cried Judy, as a shadowy figure shot past, heading back the way it had come. "There he goes again!"

From the brief glimpse they had, it looked as though Paddington was trying to keep the business end of Mr Brown's broom between his legs with one paw, whilst at the same time wave a book up and down with his other, not unlike a bird that had fallen out of its nest and was learning to fly.

A moment later there was a loud clatter from somewhere outside and a dustbin lid rolled slowly past the French windows.

Jonathan jumped to his feet. "It sounds as though he's had a crash landing," he cried.

"Are you surprised?" asked Judy. "He had his eyes closed."

"It isn't like him to go rushing around the

garden before breakfast," broke in Mrs Brown. "I do hope he's all right."

"He was as right as rain when he went to bed last night," said Judy. "I met him on the landing. He said he was going to do his accounts."

"Perhaps he found he was overdrawn," said Mr Brown. "I'd better have a quiet word with him after breakfast."

Mrs Bird gave a snort as she came into the room carrying a coffee pot. "There's nothing wrong with that bear's accounts," she said. "If you ask me, he's planning something. Earlier on he was asking me if I had any pumpkins."

"Ssh!" warned Mrs Brown. "Here he comes."

The Browns were only just in time. They had scarcely settled down, trying to look as though butter wouldn't melt in their mouths, when Paddington entered the room.

After mopping his brow several times with a napkin, he joined them at the table, and while he was unscrewing the lid on the marmalade jar they managed to get a closer look at his book.

Most of the cover was filled with the silhouette

of an elderly lady astride a broomstick. The pointed hat she wore matched her sharply pointed nose as she hovered above a row of chimney pots. Far from being called *Teach Yourself to Fly*, the book bore the words: *Everything You Need to Know about Witches, Warlocks and Hobgoblins.*

Mr Brown gave a groan. "Of course! It's October 31st."

"Halloween," said Judy.

"Trick or treat time," added Jonathan.

Paddington spread a liberal helping of marmalade on his freshly buttered toast.

"Mr Gruber lent it to me," he explained. "I haven't read anything about warlocks or hobgoblins yet, but there's a very good chapter on witches and making masks. And there's another one telling you how to decorate a patio using lanterns made out of hollowed out pumpkins. They're called jack-o'-lanterns, and if you put a lighted candle inside them it keeps evil spirits away.

"There's another chapter on superstitions," he continued. "It says if you take a three-legged stool and sit at some crossroads while the church clock strikes midnight it will tell you the names of all those who will die during the next twelve months."

"Very cheering, I must say," said Mrs Bird. "I know one thing. Anyone who sits on a stool near our crossroads at midnight could well end up top of the list."

All the same, Paddington's enthusiasm was infectious and as soon as the rest of the family finished their meal they gathered round his chair.

"I've never been to a Halloween party," he said wistfully. "I don't think they have them in Darkest Peru."

Mrs Brown caught her husband's eye. "We haven't had one for ages, Henry," she said. "It might be fun."

"Please, Dad," chorused Jonathan and Judy.

Mr Brown weakened. "Perhaps a small one," he said. "Just for the family, but no more. It's bad enough as it is with all those people ringing the front door bell and calling 'trick or treat' through the letter box. The only time I didn't answer it last year we lost our dustbin lid."

"It did get found in the canal," said Jonathan.

"I'll get some chocolate bars in," said Mrs Brown hastily. "They always go down well."

Paddington turned over the page. "There's a recipe for a witches' brew," he read.

"It's called stir-fly and it sounds very interesting."

"I think you must mean stir-*fry*, dear," said Mrs Brown. "Unless, of course, it's a misprint."

Jonathan took a closer look. "No," he said firmly. "Paddington's right. It *is* stir-*fly*."

"It gives the recipe," announced Paddington, reading from the book. "It's a mixture of toenail clippings, bats' blood and dead flies."

"Charming," said Mr Brown. "I can't wait!"

"They're not real," piped up Judy, seeing the look on everyone's face. "You can make pretend toenail clippings out of pieces of chicory, and for the flies all you need is some old currants that have gone hard. Mix it all together with tomato ketchup and Bob's your uncle."

"Bob's welcome to it, whoever he is," murmured Mr Brown. "I'm not sure I wouldn't prefer the real thing."

"Look," said Jonathan, gazing over Paddington's shoulder. "There's something here about taking a kipper to bed with you."

"That's another very good chapter," said Paddington knowledgeably. "I read it under the eiderdown last night. It says if you take a kipper to bed and eat it before you go to sleep, the person you are going to marry will bring you a glass of water during the night to quench your thirst."

"Hmmm," said Mrs Bird. "I hope whoever it turns out to be is prepared to wash the sheets in the morning, that's all I can say."

"Anyway," said Judy. "You're not thinking of getting married, are you?"

"I might do," said Paddington darkly.

"There is another way," he continued. "It says here, if you cut the letters of the alphabet out of some newspaper headlines and float them in a bowl of water they will spell out the name for you."

Mr Brown pointedly glanced at his watch, and then reached for his morning paper. "I think it's time I went to the office," he said. "It's a bit early in the day for origami."

"What a bit of luck it's half term," said Jonathan, after Mr Brown had said his goodbyes. "We can help get everything ready."

"If I were you, Paddington," said Mrs Bird, "I'd get down to the market as soon as possible. Once people begin to realise what day it is, there could be a run on pumpkins." She reached for her handbag. "While you're there you can get a box of night-lights to go inside them."

"Don't forget we need some chicory for the toenails," called Judy.

Paddington made a note of it and in no time at all he set off with his list, leaving Jonathan and Judy to start making the masks.

"Very wise," said Mrs Bird approvingly, when she saw what they were up to.

"Speaking from experience, that bear and glue pots are best kept as far apart as possible. He can help me with the pumpkins when he gets back."

"You don't think Paddington was serious about getting married, do you?" asked Judy, when she and Jonathan were on their own.

"I can't picture him carrying anyone over the threshold if that's what you mean," said Jonathan. "He'd be bound to drop them, or else get stuck halfway through the door; besides he's got to find someone first."

"It's hard to picture anyone wanting to share kippers in bed with him," said Judy, reaching for the paint. "It would be a bad start to married life. I think we're fairly safe."

By the time Paddington got back from the market, they had both made so many masks it was hard to find anywhere to sit. Having tried his paw unsuccessfully at painting one whilst standing up, Jonathan suggested he might look in the garage for some old pieces of frayed rope so that he could make a wig for himself.

Mrs Bird set to work hollowing out the pumpkins, and as soon as that job was done, having left Jonathan and Judy to put the night-lights inside them, she turned her attention to the cooking, leaving Paddington to look for some way of dyeing his wig black.

One way or another everyone was kept busy, but if the first half of the day passed quickly, waiting for it to get dark seemed to take for ever.

In order to pass the time, Paddington retired to his bedroom to write some Halloween poems while he was trying out his costume.

"I'm ready for the trick or treat part," he announced, when he came back downstairs at long last.

With the addition of a black pointed hat, similar to the one on the cover of Mr Gruber's book, everyone agreed he made a very good witch indeed. The finishing touch was a set of white fangs Judy had made for him out of some orange peel turned inside out.

"I wouldn't like to meet you on a dark night," said Jonathan, when they went out into the front garden.

"I thought perhaps we could start with Mr Curry as he's nearest," said Paddington.

"Do you think that's wise?" asked Judy.

"I've written a special poem for him," said Paddington. "I don't want to waste it."

"You must like living dangerously," said Jonathan. "I doubt if you'll get anything out of him. It would be easier to get blood out of a stone."

"Pigs might fly!" agreed Judy.

"I don't suppose he'll recognise me in my outfit," said Paddington optimistically, as he set off through the front gate leaving the others to hide behind the fence.

"I wouldn't bank on it," called Jonathan.

But he was too late, for Paddington was already out of earshot.

Having pressed Mr Curry's bell push several

times, he hid in the shadows, carefully keeping the lantern behind him so that his face wouldn't show.

"Yes?" barked the Browns' neighbour, as he opened the door a fraction and peered through the gap. "Who is it?"

"Hurry, hurry, Mr Curry," called Paddington, disguising his voice. "Give me a gift, and I'll be swift."

"Go away, bear!" exclaimed Mr Curry. "How dare you! Any more of that nonsense and I shall call the police." And with that he slammed the door in Paddington's face.

"That settles it," said Jonathan, when they heard what had happened. "It's time for tricks, not treats.

"I found a good one in your book while you were in the garage this morning. You tie one end of a length of cord to someone's front door knob. Then you pull it tight and tie the other end to a convenient tree.

"After that, you ring the front door bell and hide. If it's done properly, when they try to open the door they think it's stuck. I've brought some cord in case it was needed."

"It'll serve him right for being so mean," said Judy.

"I'll do it," said Paddington eagerly. "Bears are good at knots."

He seemed so keen on the idea the others didn't have the heart to say 'no'. Instead, they kept watch while he hurried back to Mr Curry's house armed with the cord.

Tying it to the door knob took rather longer than he had bargained for, especially as he was trying to do it as quietly as possible, and it wasn't until he looked round for something he could tie the other end to that he realised Mr Curry's front garden was like the proverbial desert. There wasn't a sign of a convenient shrub, let alone a tree.

Paddington was about to go back home and ask Jonathan's advice when the door suddenly opened.

"Who's that rattling my letter box?" barked Mr Curry.

"I might have known!" he growled, when he caught sight of Paddington hiding behind his pumpkin. "Up to your tricks again, bear!"

"Oh, no," said Paddington hastily. "They're not *my* tricks, Mr Curry. They're in Mr Gruber's book... I mean..."

The Browns' neighbour stared at him suspiciously. "What's that in your paw?" he demanded.

"It's my jack-o'-lantern," explained Paddington. He held the pumpkin up for Mr Curry to see. "It's supposed to frighten off evil spirits, but it doesn't seem to be working very well..." He broke off as he caught sight of the look on the other's face.

"I meant, what's in your *other* paw?" barked Mr Curry. "The one behind your back." And before Paddington could stop him he had grabbed hold of the cord.

"I wouldn't pull it if I were you, Mr Curry," said Paddington anxiously.

"Nonsense!" barked the Browns' neighbour. "There's only one way to find out where something goes – that's to give it a good tug." And without further ado he wound the cord round his other hand and pulled.

There was a loud bang as his door slammed shut. It was followed almost immediately by a sound of tinkling as a metal object landed on the path at their feet.

Mr Curry stared it. "That looks like a door knob," he growled. "Have you any idea how it got there, bear? It might have caused a nasty accident."

Paddington held out his lantern and took a closer look. "I don't think it's one of ours, Mr Curry," he said. "Mrs Bird always keeps our door knobs polished."

"That still doesn't explain what it's doing there," growled Mr Curry.

"I was looking for a convenient tree..." explained Paddington.

"I don't have any trees," growled Mr Curry. "Nasty, untidy things, dropping their leaves everywhere."

"I know," said Paddington unhappily. "That's why the door knob trick didn't work properly. Yours must have fallen off by mistake. It wasn't meant to."

"I'll give you tricks, bear," barked Mr Curry. "They ought not to be allowed. If I had my way I'd..." he broke off.

"Would you mind repeating what you've just said?"

Mr Curry's face had grown purple with rage. In fact, Paddington didn't like the look of it at all and he hastily lowered his lantern to be on the safe side.

"If you don't mind," he said, "I'd rather not."

But the Browns' neighbour was already doing it for him. "Are you trying to tell me that's *my* door knob, bear?" he spluttered.

Clearly hardly able to believe his eyes, let alone his ears, he gazed at his front door, then looked at the end of the cord tied round the knob.

"Do you realise," he bellowed, "you have locked me out of my own house!"

"No, Mr Curry," said Paddington, glad to be on firm ground at last. "*I* didn't lock you out. You did it yourself. It's what Mrs Bird calls a self-inflicted wound. She often says you're very good at those."

Raising his hat politely, he looked anxiously over his shoulder, but Jonathan and Judy were too well hidden to be of any help. "I think perhaps I'd better go now," he said. "We're having a Halloween party and I don't want to be late."

Mr Curry paused from whatever it was he had been about to say and a cunning gleam came into his eyes. "Is that so, bear?" he said. "I thought I saw you doing a lot of coming and going this morning."

"There was a lot to get ready," said Paddington, only too pleased to change the subject. "Mrs Bird's been very busy, baking cakes, and making some special stir-fly mixture."

"Seeing I have been locked out of my house," said Mr Curry, "it couldn't have happened at a better time. It's very kind of you to invite me, bear. Unless, of course," he added meaningly, "you would rather I told the Browns what you've just done."

Jonathan stood up. "That's torn it!" he said gloomily, overhearing the conversation. "Wait until Dad hears what's happened. He won't be pleased. Mr Curry is the last person he'll want to see when he gets home."

"Paddington wasn't joking when he said bears are good at knots," agreed Judy. "How's he going to get out of this one?"

"I bet he finds a way," said Jonathan loyally. "He usually comes out on top."

Mr Curry gazed round the Browns' living room as he made himself comfortable in Mr Brown's favourite armchair. Having helped himself liberally from a bowl of chocolates he gave a shiver and then stood up again.

"I think I'll move nearer the fire," he said. "I got cold standing outside."

Much to everyone's dismay he looked all set for the rest of the evening.

"Now, bear," he said, addressing Paddington. "It's my turn. Seeing you have kindly invited me to your party, I have a poem for *you*.

"You mentioned something just now about having some stir-fry… so first of all, trick or treat, give me some of that to eat!"

Mrs Bird pursed her lips, but before she had time to say anything Paddington jumped to his feet. "Don't worry, Mrs Bird," he called, as he hurried out of the room. "Leave it to me."

It wasn't long before he returned carrying a large bowl and a spoon on a tray.

Mr Curry scooped up the last of the chocolates and placed them inside his jacket pocket before turning his attention to Paddington's offering.

"You cannot say I do not try," said Paddington. "I'll give it to you, then I must fly."

"Thank you, bear," said Mr Curry, licking his lips. And without further ado he grabbed the spoon and began attacking the bowl.

Paddington waited until the Browns' neighbour had finished his second mouthful and was visibly slowing down. "I'm afraid it's a bit chewy," he said. "It's a special Halloween recipe."

"Most unusual," said Mr Curry. "I've never had anything quite like it before. Aren't you having any, bear?"

"I don't think so, Mr Curry," said Paddington. "Thank you very much. My Aunt Lucy always told me never to swallow flies. It's a bit difficult in Darkest Peru. They have a lot of them there. She had to keep her jars covered whenever she was making marmalade in case some went in. They're supposed to make you go thin."

Mr Curry gave a snort. "Nonsense!" he barked. "That's an old wives' tale if ever I heard one. Besides, what's that got to do with…?" He broke off, the spoon halfway to his mouth.

"Why are you telling me that, bear?"

"I thought you might be interested," said Paddington innocently. "I did give your bowl a good stir before I brought it in."

Mr Curry jumped to his feet. "Bear!" he bellowed.

"Are you trying to tell me I've been eating… stirred *flies*?"

"May I get you another helping?" asked Mrs Bird sweetly, before Paddington had a chance to answer.

"No, you may not!" spluttered Mr Curry. Clutching his stomach, he gave a loud groan. "That's the very last time I accept an invitation to one of your parties, bear!"

"Could we have that in writing?" murmured Jonathan, fortunately not loud enough for anyone other than Judy to hear.

"Accept an invitation indeed!" said Mrs Bird. "I heard you browbeating Paddington just now. As for being locked out of your house – you know very well we keep a spare key for you in case of an emergency. Come with me."

And while Paddington took the remains of Mr Curry's soup into the kitchen, Mrs Bird led their uninvited guest into the hall.

Moments later, for the second time that evening the sound of a front door being slammed echoed round Windsor Gardens.

"Who would have believed it?" said Mrs Brown.

"I told you Paddington would find a way," said Jonathan.

"Still waters run deep," said Judy.

"There's nothing still about that bear's waters," said Mrs Bird, as she came back into the room. "If you ask me, there's a lot goes on under that hat we don't know about."

"Would anyone else like any stirred flies?" she

asked. "Or would you prefer pumpkin soup? I made it specially. You can't make lanterns without having a lot of the inside fruit left over."

"It's very good," said Paddington, licking his lips as he arrived back from the kitchen. "I've just been testing it."

"In that case," said Mr Brown. "Come on, everyone… It's party time!"

Afterwards they all voted it was the best soup they'd had for a long time.

"Aren't you going to take your hat off, Paddington?" asked Mrs Brown, when it was time to go to bed.

"If you don't," said Mrs Bird, "the glue may melt during the night, then you'll be stuck with it."

Paddington considered the matter for a moment or two before he went upstairs. He felt very torn. "I suppose I'd better," he said at long last, "otherwise I shan't be able to raise it if I meet someone I know when I'm out shopping. But if you don't mind I'll take my lantern with me while the night-light is still burning. It's been such a nice Halloween I don't want to miss a minute of it."

"I know I've said it before," said Mrs Bird, as Paddington disappeared up the stairs, "but I'll say it again. That bear takes the biscuit!"

Chapter Five

PADDINGTON SPILLS THE BEANS

ONE BRIGHT DECEMBER morning Paddington decided to make himself useful in the garden. With Christmas not far away he was anxious to earn some extra pocket money, so he set to work at the front of the house, clearing up the last of the autumn leaves and generally tidying up the flower beds.

He didn't want a repeat of the previous year's debacle, when he gave everyone in the family a diary he'd come across on a stall in the market. Like most bears, he had an eye for a bargain, and at the time five for the price of one sounded very good value indeed.

It wasn't until halfway through Boxing Day afternoon, when Mr Brown laid down his pen at long last, having finished the arduous task of transferring all the names and addresses and birthday reminders from his old diary into the new one, that he happened to glance at the date and discovered the two were identical.

Having swept the leaves into a tidy pile, Paddington took some secateurs out of his duffle coat pocket and turned his attention to the rose bushes in case they needed a final prune before winter set in.

A quick glance decided him against it. The roses were Mr Brown's pride and joy and he went to great pains to ensure they were pruned close to an outward-facing bud.

Whenever Paddington looked at them the only

buds he could find always seemed to face the wrong way, and that day was no exception.

He was in the middle of taking a closer look at one of the stems through his magnifying glass when he heard a cough. Looking round he realised he was being watched.

"Ahem," said a man, looking over the railings. "Forgive me. I can see you're busy. Please don't bother to stand up."

Paddington looked most offended. "I *am* standing up," he announced.

"Oh!" The newcomer sounded rather flustered. "I do beg your pardon, but I assumed you were a jobbing gardener; a refugee from some foreign clime, perhaps?

"I wonder… are your employers at home?"

"My *employers*!" repeated Paddington, growing more and more upset. "But I *live* here. I'm trying to make my ends meet in time for Christmas. I was looking for some outward-facing buds, but I can't find any."

"I know just how you feel," said the man sympathetically.

He held up a clipboard. "I'm trying to conduct a survey, but so far I haven't found a single person to interview. Everybody in the road seems to be out."

"I expect it's because of your board," said Paddington knowledgeably. "Mrs Bird says she never opens the door to a man with a clipboard. It usually means they're after something."

"Ah!" The man gave a hollow laugh. "Thank you very much for the tip. I'm not used to this kind of work, you see, and…" His voice trailed away under Paddington's gaze.

"Since you live here," he continued, "perhaps you wouldn't mind answering a few simple questions. It will only take up a minute or two of your valuable time. We are asking people about their views…"

"I have a very good one from my bedroom window," said Paddington, only too happy to oblige. "On a clear day I can see the British Telecom Tower."

The interviewer allowed himself a smile. "How very interesting." He took a closer look at

Paddington. "Forgive my mentioning it, but from your accent I take it you are not... well... I mean, where exactly are you from?"

"Peru," said Paddington. "*Darkest* Peru."

"Darkest Peru?" repeated the man. "I've come across a good many Bulgarians and Poles coming over here to work, but I've never met anyone from Darkest Peru before." He consulted a sheet of paper on his clipboard. "There isn't even a box I can tick. If you don't mind my saying so, I hope there isn't a flood this winter."

"Mr Curry had one last year," said Paddington.

"He did?" exclaimed the man excitedly. He jotted the name down. "Perhaps you could give me his address. I'll see if I can jog his memory."

"I would rather you didn't," said Paddington anxiously. "He's our next-door neighbour and we don't get on very well."

"Oh, dear," said the man. "Does it bring back unhappy memories for you?"

"No," said Paddington. "But it does for Mr Curry. He had a burst pipe in his bathroom and I was helping him mend it.

"He gave me a hammer to hold and told me that when he nodded his head I was to hit it. So I did. I didn't realise he meant the pipe."

"I see the problem," agreed the man. "It's not something you would forget in a hurry."

He turned over the page. "Changing the subject, do you have any complaints about the way you have been treated since you arrived in this country?"

Paddington considered the matter for a moment. "Well, it wasn't Mrs Bird's fault," he said, "but my boiled egg was a bit runny this morning."

"Your boiled egg was a bit runny?" The man had started to write something down, but he crossed it out. "I hardly think that's a reasonable cause for complaint."

"It is if you're a bear," said Paddington hotly. "If you're a bear and the yolk dries on your whiskers it makes them stick together and it's very painful. It hurts every time you open your mouth."

"Er, yes," said the interviewer, "I suppose it would. Did you register a complaint?"

Paddington looked taken aback at the thought.

"I wouldn't dare," he said. "Mrs Bird rules the house with a rod of iron."

"Really?" The man looked round nervously. "Does she carry it with her?"

"Oh, it's only a pretend one," said Paddington. "But she can be a bit fierce at times. Mr Brown says that deep down she has a heart of gold. Anyway, she's out with Mrs Brown doing the Christmas shopping, and both Jonathan and Judy are away at school. They're not due home until tomorrow, so I've been left in charge."

The man looked relieved. "This Mrs Bird," he said. "I would like to know more about her. Do I take it she isn't a very good cook?"

"*Not a very good cook*?" repeated Paddington indignantly. "Mrs Bird's dumplings are the best I've ever tasted. They're well known in the neighbourhood."

"Dumplings well known in neighbourhood," repeated the man, making an entry on his form.

"So is her marmalade," said Paddington. "It's full of chunks."

Feeling under his hat, he produced a sandwich. "You can try this one if you like. I made it myself the week before last."

It looked somewhat the worse for wear, and the man eyed it doubtfully. "I think I would rather not," he said.

"I always keep one under my hat in case of an emergency," explained Paddington, "but nothing's gone wrong for several weeks now."

"I don't suppose you happen to keep one of Mrs

Bird's dumplings under there as well, do you?" asked the man. "I could take a picture of it on my mobile."

"A *dumpling*!" exclaimed Paddington. "Under my hat!" He gave the interviewer a very hard stare indeed.

The man's voice trailed away as he caught the look on Paddington's face. "May I ask how you got here in the first place?" he enquired, hurriedly changing the subject.

"I came in a small boat," said Paddington. "I was a stowaway."

"All the way from Darkest Peru?" The interviewer raised his eyebrows. "I know a lot of you boat people are desperate, but that sounds like a world record to me. Your paws must have been sore after all that rowing."

"Oh, I didn't have to row," said Paddington. "The boat was fixed to the side of a big ship. It was my Aunt Lucy's idea. I was a stowaway."

"All the same," said the man, "it can't have been easy."

"It certainly wasn't in the Bay of Biscuits," said Paddington. "I had a job to stand up. The sea was so rough I nearly got washed overboard several times."

"Surely you mean the Bay of Biscay?" said the man.

"I called it the Bay of Biscuits," said Paddington firmly. "Someone was hanging over the ship's rails and they let go of a Garibaldi by mistake. It landed on my head, so I had it for dinner. I felt much better afterwards."

"How many B's are there in Garibaldi?" asked the man as he wrote it down.

"There aren't bees in a Garibaldi," said Paddington. "They have currants instead."

Taking a deep breath, the interviewer reached for his eraser. "This Aunt Lucy of yours," he continued. "Can you tell me more about her?"

"Well," said Paddington. "She's very wise. If it wasn't for her I wouldn't be here at all. Besides, she taught me all I know."

"Perhaps you could let me have her address," said the man. "I'd like to take her on board and make her part of my team. She sounds just the kind of person we're looking for."

"I don't think that would be very easy," said Paddington. "She's living in the Home for Retired Bears in Lima. Besides, she doesn't play any ball games."

The interviewer gave Paddington a glassy stare as he reached for his eraser again.

"I had a clean form when I started out this morning," he said plaintively. "Now look at it!

"I suppose," he continued, trying another tack, "since your Aunt Lucy is in a home, she's… er… I mean, is there an uncle by any chance?"

"Oh, yes," said Paddington. "Uncle Pastuzo. But we haven't seen him since the earthquake…"

"You mean you're an earthquake victim…" The man's pen fairly raced across the page. "Tell me more…"

"Well," said Paddington, "there's not much to tell. I was fast asleep in a tree at the time. There was a loud rumble and the earth began to shake. When I woke up everything looked different. Everyone else apart from Aunt Lucy had disappeared."

"Even your Uncle Pastuzo?" said the interviewer.

"Especially Uncle Pastuzo," said Paddington. "I think he must have known it was going to happen because he went out early that day. But he left his old hat and a suitcase with a secret compartment behind, along with a note to say I could have them if anything happened to him."

"And you have never heard any more of him since?"

Paddington shook his head sadly. "That's why Aunt Lucy brought me up. She taught me my tables, and she taught me to say 'please' and 'thank you' when I'm out shopping, and to raise my hat whenever I meet someone I know.

"She also taught me to count my blessings when things look black. It's the first thing she does when she wakes in the morning. She says nine times out of ten you have more than you think you have."

"Would there were more about like her," said the man. He turned the page. "One last thing before I leave you in peace. What are your feelings about being a blood donor?"

"No, thank you," said Paddington firmly. "I haven't had my elevenses yet and it might make me go wibbly woo."

"I shouldn't let that worry you," said the man. "You can lie down afterwards, *and* they give you a nice cup of tea into the bargain."

"I prefer cocoa," said Paddington. "Bears do, you know."

"No, I didn't know that," said the man, entering the information on his form.

"While we are on the subject of medical matters," he continued, "if you don't fancy being a blood donor, how about donating one of your organs when the time comes?"

Paddington considered the matter for a moment or two. He wondered if he ought to mention Jonathan's mouth organ. It had been a nine days' wonder at the time and everybody had breathed a sigh of relief when he took it back to school with him after the holidays.

"I don't have any myself," he said.

The man concealed a smile. "Oh, but you must have," he said. "Everyone has organs."

"Mr Curry doesn't for a start," said Paddington.

"Oh, dear," said the interviewer. "Poor man. What with that *and* having his pipes frozen, he must be in a terrible state. I dare say he has to be tended day and night."

Paddington looked over his shoulder. "I don't think so," he said, lowering his voice. "He lives all by himself."

The man followed the direction of Paddington's gaze. "It gets worse and worse," he said. "Is that why the curtains are drawn?"

"Mrs Bird says it's because he doesn't like people spying on him," said Paddington.

"I'm not surprised," said the man, "if he has no organs."

"Jonathan had one once," said Paddington. "But he swapped it with a boy at school for a pencil box."

The interviewer's eyes nearly popped out of their sockets. "Jonathan swapped one of his organs for a pencil box?" he repeated. "Do you know which one it was?"

"I don't know the name," said Paddington. "But it was very special. It had two tiers. One for ordinary pencils and another one for crayons."

"I don't mean the pencil box," said the man. "I

mean which organ. This could be headline news! It's just the kind of material my editor is looking for."

"Oh, dear!" Paddington suddenly wondered if he had said the right thing.

"Are you absolutely certain you don't want to set an example?" said the man. "I wasn't meaning today, of course. It won't happen until after you…" he shifted uneasily underneath Paddington's hard stare. "Well, you know… after you er, um."

"After I er, um?" repeated Paddington.

"That's right," said the man. "It happens to us all at some time."

"It hasn't happened to me yet," said Paddington.

"I can see that," said the man, looking as though he was beginning to wish it had.

"One last thing," he remarked casually. "Can you tell me the name of Jonathan's school?"

"I'm very sorry," said Paddington, raising his hat politely to show the conversation was at an end. "I'm afraid I can't."

"What's it worth?" asked the interviewer. Taking out his wallet, he fingered some notes.

"More than all the tea in China," said Paddington, remembering one of Mrs Bird's favourite phrases.

"And if this doesn't work?" asked the man, detaching one of the notes, crackling it enticingly between his thumb and forefinger.

"I have a secret weapon," said Paddington. "I'll show you if you like…"

Looking round to make sure nobody was watching, he gave the interviewer one of his hardest stares ever.

The man shuddered as though he had been struck by lightning, and something fell to the ground.

"That's another thing Aunt Lucy taught me," said Paddington. "It comes in very useful at times!"

"I think I might call it a day," said the man, hastily retrieving his pen. He handed the note across the railings. "You'd better have this anyway. It may help you to make your ends meet before Christmas.

"We're giving them away this week," he added. "It's a 'Thank You' present."

And with that he turned on his heels and

disappeared down Windsor Gardens as though he had a train to catch.

Paddington gazed at the note for a moment or two. It didn't look like any sort of money he had seen before. Instead of the £ sign, there was a picture of an aeroplane, followed by a lot of words in small print. None of them seemed to make any sense, so he slipped it into his duffle coat pocket for safe keeping and hurried back into the house in case anyone else came along wanting to interview him.

"What do you think 'er, ums' are?" asked Mr Brown.

It was the following day, and he had just arrived back from the station having collected Jonathan and Judy, who were home for the Christmas holiday.

"You've been reading Paddington's postcard, Henry," said Mrs Brown accusingly.

"I couldn't help it," said Mr Brown. "It was lying on the hall table ready to be posted. Anyway, it sounds as though you've read it too."

"It's addressed to his Aunt Lucy," said Mrs

Brown. "I have no idea what it means, but he told her not to worry."

"If you ask me," said Mrs Bird, "a spoonful of castor oil might not come amiss."

"Poor old Paddington," said Judy.

"Worse things happen at sea," said Jonathan cheerfully.

"I don't know about that," said Mr Brown. "Look at this headline!"

He held up the front page of a local newspaper.

ORGAN REPLACEMENT SCANDAL ROCKS LONDON'S WEST END

"I can't say I've felt any tremors," said Mrs Bird, reading it out loud.

"I don't know where they get all these stories from in the first place," agreed Mrs Brown. "I can't believe half of them are true. It doesn't sound like anywhere round here, thank goodness!"

"I wouldn't be too sure," warned Mr Brown. "It's the same postcode as ours – W11."

He continued reading. "'Where will it all end?' asks our man on the spot. Posing as an interviewer, our intrepid reporter, Mervyn Doom, managed to

infiltrate the gang and obtain in-depth information from one of its hammer-carrying members."

"He makes it sound like some kind of ball game," interrupted Mrs Brown. "Where on earth did you get the paper?"

"On Paddington station while I was waiting for the train," said Mr Brown.

"Apparently the person he interviewed was disguised as a jobbing gardener. He gave the game away by saying he was looking for some outward-facing rosebuds, not realising it was long past the normal pruning season."

He looked up from the paper. "Can you imagine? It shows the type of person the authorities are up against.

"During the course of the interview our informant also let slip the fact that an undercover trade in organ transplants is rife.

"A local schoolboy swapped one of his for a pencil box – the name of the boy and the school have been withheld for legal reasons. Meanwhile, in this outwardly respectable neighbourhood, others – bereft of everything that makes them tick – lie behind drawn curtains waiting for help."

"What *is* the world coming to?" exclaimed Mrs Bird.

"And another thing," continued Mr Brown, "according to this paper the gates are about to open on a flood of boat people from Peru.

"Our question is WHEN WILL SOMETHING BE DONE ABOUT IT?

"THERE IS NO TIME TO BE LOST!"

"Does it say who's behind it?" asked Mrs Brown.

"Apparently the Gang-master-in-chief is a woman," said Mr Brown. "Notorious for her dumplings, and wielding an iron bar, she so terrifies those around her the subject of the interview is forced to hide his marmalade sandwiches under his hat."

The Browns looked at one another. Suddenly, it was all starting to sound much closer to home than they had thought.

"You don't think…" began Mr Brown.

"Oh dear, Henry," said Mrs Brown. "I'm very much afraid I do."

"He asked if he could borrow your secateurs yesterday morning," said Mrs Bird.

"He wanted to do some work in the front garden."

"Don't tell me he was having a go at my roses?" exclaimed Mr Brown, the full seriousness of the situation suddenly coming home to him.

"I don't like the sound of that last bit," said Mrs Bird. "If the 'powers that be' get hold of the story there's no knowing what will happen. We can await the ring on the front door bell."

The Browns exchanged anxious glances. In the beginning Paddington had just sort of happened, but over the years he had become so much a part of the family they couldn't picture life without him. They had certainly never thought of him as being a refugee; still less the possibility of his being an illegal one.

"I think 'they've' started doing something about things already," said Jonathan. "I saw an ambulance outside Mr Curry's house soon after we got back. There was a terrible row going on. They were trying to tie him on to a stretcher."

"I suppose they might declare Paddington *persona non grata*," said Mr Brown.

"That means an unwelcome person," said Judy, for her brother's benefit.

"Thanks a heap!" said Jonathan. "Who got an A Star in his GCSE?"

"Anyway," said Judy, "he's not a person. He's a bear."

"*And* he's always welcome," chimed in Mrs Bird. "If anyone tries to take him away after all this time they'll have me to deal with."

"Who in the world would want to report him?" asked Judy.

"I imagine Mr Curry for a start," said Jonathan, "if Paddington had anything to do with what happened this morning. Perhaps we could hide him under the floorboards – like the French did with escaped prisoners during the last war."

"I shall never go out and leave that bear alone again," said Mrs Bird.

"I'm sure he meant well," said Mrs Brown.

"They can't," said Judy. "Take him away, I mean."

"There's no such word in the English language as 'can't'," said Mrs Bird grimly.

"What shall we tell Paddington?" broke in Mr Brown, lowering his voice.

"For the time being," said Mrs Bird, "I suggest we don't tell him anything. He'll be most upset if he thinks the whole thing is his fault."

"He really will have trouble with his 'er, ums' then," said Jonathan.

"Careful," hissed Judy, "I think he's coming downstairs. I was wondering where he'd got to."

Sure enough, a moment later the door opened

and a familiar face appeared round the gap.

"Can anyone tell me what Air Miles are?" asked Paddington.

"Well," said Mr Brown, after he had gone. "That was a conversation stopper if ever I heard one. I wonder what he's up to now?"

"I shudder to think," said Mrs Brown.

"Time alone will tell," said Mrs Bird. "I dare say we shall know soon enough."

Chapter Six

PADDINGTON AIMS HIGH

THE FOLLOWING MORNING, blissfully unaware of the
dark cloud which had settled over number thirty-two
Windsor Gardens, Paddington set out soon after breakfast.

Heading in the opposite direction to the one he
normally took, he made his way uphill towards a shop
he remembered seeing on one of his outings with
Mr Gruber.

It was situated in a busy high street some distance from the Portobello Market, and it stuck in his mind, partly because at the time he had thought Oyster Travels seemed a very unusual name for a shop, and also because there had been a large revolving globe in the window. Mr Gruber had stopped to admire it, and as it went slowly round and round he had pointed out all the different countries as they went past.

"Since they invented the aeroplane, Mr Brown," he had said, "the world has shrunk. There are very few places left that cannot be reached in a matter of hours rather than weeks. I expect this shop took its name from the old saying: 'the world is your oyster'. In other words, 'it is yours to enjoy'."

Mr Gruber had a happy knack of making even quite ordinary things sound exciting, and Paddington's latest idea was far from ordinary. It had come to him during the night while he had been lying awake trying to think what to get the Browns for Christmas.

The first time he had seen the shop it had been

full of people, but as he drew near he was pleased to see that apart from a rather superior-looking man who looked as though he was about to open up for business, there was nobody else around.

"The early bird catches the worm," the man said approvingly, as he held the door open for Paddington.

"I dare say you'll be after one of our cheap day return trips," he said, sizing up his first customer of the day. "A day out in Brightsea, perhaps? It can be very invigorating at this time of the year. The coach leaves in half an hour, and if the weather forecast is anything to go by it will certainly blow the cobwebs out of your whiskers."

Paddington took a quick look at his reflection in the polished glass. "Those aren't cobwebs," he said, giving the man a hard stare. "It's Shredded Wheat. I ate my breakfast in a hurry because I wanted to get here before anyone else."

"I do beg your pardon." The man wilted under Paddington's gaze.

"I was really wanting to enquire about some of the places you have on your globe," said

Paddington. "Mr Gruber was telling me all about them."

"My dear sir, you couldn't have come to a better place." Leaping into action, the man began washing his hands in invisible soap as he ushered Paddington to a stool opposite one of the counters.

"I happen to be the manager," he continued, going round to the other side and reaching for a pad and pencil. "As I like to tell all our customers, the world is not only our oyster, it is yours too. We are here to take care of your every need.

"Perhaps you could let me have a few details first, starting with your name and address…"

Paddington did as he was bidden, and while the manager was writing it down he glanced around the shop. It seemed full of interesting things. Apart from a number of real oyster shells dotted around the counter, there were some giant plastic ones hanging from the ceiling, and the walls were covered in posters showing holiday-makers with happy, smiling faces as they bathed in the blue sea or lay back in their deck chairs enjoying the sunshine. There wasn't a gloomy face to be seen

anywhere, and he felt more certain than ever that he had come to the right place.

"Will it be just for your good self?" enquired the manager, "Or will you be accompanied? We do have what we call our 'Singles Special'."

"There will be seven of us," said Paddington. "It's

my treat, and I want to take them somewhere special for Christmas."

"Seven!" The manager took a firmer grip of his pencil. "Would you mind giving me their names?"

"Well," said Paddington, "there will be Mr and Mrs Brown, and Mrs Bird, Jonathan and Judy, and I'm hoping Mr Gruber might be able to come too."

"Quite a large party," said the manager, looking suitably impressed. Taking a closer look at Paddington, he revised his first impression. Clearly, he was dealing with a seasoned traveller, and an important one at that. Although the customer had arrived on foot, he wondered for a moment if he could be dealing with a television personality planning a forthcoming programme, or perhaps some kind of foreign dignitary; a slightly eccentric Indian prince down on his luck, for example. He had never met one wearing a duffle coat before, but there was a first time for everything and one never knew these days. It paid to be careful.

"I know it's a little early in the day," he said, "but would you care for a glass of champagne while we go through the possibilities?"

"No, thank you," said Paddington. "I had one once and it tickled my whiskers. I would sooner have a cup of cocoa."

The manager's face fell. "I'm afraid we shall have to wait until our Miss Pringle arrives," he said, looking at his watch. "She usually collects the milk on her way in.

"We were rushed off our feet yesterday," he explained, "what with everyone wanting to make a quick getaway for the Christmas holiday. I told the staff they could come in half an hour later than usual…" He reached out towards a rack laden with coloured brochures.

"Have you ever thought about visiting South America? The Peruvian Andes, for example? We have a tour which includes a boat trip on Lake Titicaca. As I'm sure you know, it's the highest one in the world."

"If we go to Peru," said Paddington, "I would sooner visit the Home for Retired Bears in Lima. I haven't seen my Aunt Lucy for a long time and it will be a nice surprise for her."

The manager scanned through the brochure.

"I'm afraid it doesn't mention anything about a Home for Retired Bears," he said, "but I'm sure our tour guide will be more than willing to offer advice when you get there.

"Alternatively," he reached for another brochure, "how would you feel about visiting India?" He held it aloft for Paddington's benefit. "Have you ever seen the Taj Mahal by moonlight?"

Paddington peered at the picture. "No," he said, "but last year I was taken to see the Christmas lights at Crumbold and Ferns."

"If I may be so bold," said the manager, "there is simply no comparison. In fact, the two can hardly be mentioned in the same breath."

"I didn't have to wait for a full moon to see Crumbold and Ferns' lights," said Paddington firmly. "They were on day and night. *And* they kept changing colour. Besides, I usually go to bed early."

"If you spend more than two nights in India," said the manager, not to be outdone, "I could make sure you get a free elephant ride thrown in."

"I don't think Mrs Bird would be very keen on

that," replied Paddington. "She likes a wheel at all four corners."

"I can see I am dealing with a young gentleman of taste and discernment," said the manager, trying to mask his disappointment. "Perhaps I might tempt you with something nearer home. How about a visit to Italy and the Leaning Tower of Pisa?"

"I don't think Mrs Bird would like that very much either," said Paddington. "She was very worried last year when Mr Brown found a crack in the kitchen ceiling."

"Perhaps, before you reach a final decision you might care to bring the lady in?" suggested the manager. "I shall be more than happy to go through the itinerary with her."

"It's meant to be a surprise," said Paddington, "and Mrs Bird doesn't like surprises."

"Oh, dear," said the manager through gritted teeth. "I trust she doesn't object to flying."

"When we went to France by aeroplane," said Paddington, "she kept her eyes closed during take off and landing. She said if God had meant us to fly he would have given us wings."

"Ah," said the manager, looking slightly dazed. "I suppose the dear lady does have a point."

He tried dipping his toes in the water again. "Would Sir be thinking of travelling First or Club Class?"

"Whichever you think is best," said Paddington. "I want it to be a special treat."

"It depends a little on the overall cost," said the manager, trying to sum up his client.

"I'm not worried about the money," said Paddington.

"Then undoubtedly First Class is best," said the manager. "I can thoroughly recommend it. It's much more restful."

"We shall need five separate rooms," said Paddington.

"They aren't exactly what you might call rooms," said the manager. "Not even on the biggest planes, unless you happen to be travelling as a guest of the United States' President. But these days the seats do fold right back, and apart from the noise of the engines, once they turn the lights out you can almost believe you are in a room."

"Mrs Bird would like that," said Paddington. "Especially if they switch the lights off."

The manager breathed a sigh of relief. "In that case," he said, washing his hands in invisible soap again, "it sounds as though our 'Gold Star, top of the range Round the World Special' would suit you down to the ground. You will be fully escorted all the way and you will stay at all the best five star hotels; even Mrs Bird would be hard put to find fault with the service…"

"It sounds very good value," broke in Paddington. "I think I would like one of those, please."

"In which case," said the manager, "if you intend travelling over the Christmas period we had better strike while the iron is hot before everything gets booked up. Excuse me for a moment."

Handing Paddington some brochures to read while he was waiting, he turned to a nearby computer and began running his hands over the keys with practised ease. Several minutes passed before he pressed a button and almost immediately a long roll of paper began to emerge.

"There you are," he said, holding the end of it up for Paddington to see. "The wonders of science! Everything you want has been confirmed. It is all down in print, including the grand total."

"Thank you very much," said Paddington, as he got up to leave. "I shall always come here in future whenever I want to go anywhere."

He reached out to take the roll of paper, but the manager kept a firm hold of the other end.

"Call me old fashioned," he said, choosing his words with care, "and I sincerely hope you won't mind my mentioning it, but we at Oyster Travel believe in treating our customers as though they were part of one big, happy family.

"To put it another way, if I may make so bold, there is the small matter of a payment in advance. You will see the total amount on the end of the form."

Paddington nearly fell off his stool as he gazed at the figure on the sheet. Far from being a small matter, it struck him as a very large one. In fact, he couldn't remember ever having seen quite so many noughts in one long line before, and he was glad he didn't have to find the money.

Reaching into his duffle coat pocket, he produced the note the man conducting the survey had given him and handed it across the counter.

The manager stared at it for several seconds, hardly able to believe his eyes. Meanwhile, the smile on his face became fixed as though it had been etched in stone.

"An Air Mile!" he exclaimed at last. "*One Air Mile*! They won't even let you on the airport bus for that! Have you not read the small print on the back?"

"I tried to," said Paddington, "but it was a bit too small, even with my magnifying glass."

Gazing heavenwards the manager placed both hands together to form a steeple. He closed his eyes and his lips began to move as though he was very slowly counting, although no sound emerged.

After the speed at which he had operated the computer it struck Paddington as very strange and he wondered if the man was having trouble with all the noughts.

"Can I help?" he asked. "Bears are good at sums."

The man's lips stopped moving and he sat very still for a moment or two longer before opening his eyes.

"I have been counting up to ten," he explained, staring glassily at Paddington as though examining something the cat had brought in. "Having got as far as five, I am now going to close my eyes and begin again. If you are still here when I open them I shall not be responsible for my actions. I hope I make myself clear.

"On your way!"

Paddington didn't wait to hear any more. Without even asking for his voucher back, he made for the door.

On his way out he bumped into a lady about to enter. Raising his hat politely, he held it open for her and as he did he saw she was carrying several cartons of milk.

"If I were you, Miss Pringle," he said, "I wouldn't go anywhere near the man in charge. I don't think he's in a very good mood this morning."

Once he was outside, Paddington disappeared back down the hill as fast as his legs would carry him. He was vaguely aware of the sound of a car horn and someone shouting, but he didn't slow down until the green front door of number thirty-two Windsor Gardens had slammed shut behind him. Even then he slid one of the bolts across, just in case.

"Where *have* you been?" said Judy, as she helped him off with his duffle coat. "We've been looking for you everywhere."

While he was getting his breath back Paddington did his best to explain.

"Oh, dear," said Judy. "Poor you! But never mind. It was a lovely thought and that's what counts the most. Besides, if we *had* gone away you'd have missed Mrs Bird's turkey. Who knows what we might have ended up eating instead?

"Anyway," she handed Paddington a half opened package with a Peruvian stamp on it, "it's your Christmas parcel from Aunt Lucy and I'm afraid it got stuck in the letter box."

Paddington stared at a battered Advent calendar inside the paper. It was resting on top of some table mats.

Every Christmas without fail, a parcel arrived from the Home for Retired Bears in Lima containing presents for all the family. It was one of the many ways in which the residents whiled away their time. If it wasn't jam making, it was knitting balaclava helmets, or weaving table mats.

Mrs Bird would never have said anything for fear of hurting Paddington's feelings, but the mats were nothing if not long wearing, and over the years she had filled several kitchen drawers with them.

In any case, the most important item was always the calendar specially made by Aunt Lucy herself for Paddington.

"All my doors have come open!" he exclaimed hotly.

"It wasn't the postman's fault," said Judy. "For some reason there were more mats than usual, and when he tried getting it through the letter box it stuck halfway."

"Perhaps I could glue them shut," said Paddington hopefully.

"You'll never get them open again if you do," said Mrs Bird, joining in the conversation. "Leave it with me. I'll give it a good going-over while I'm doing the ironing."

"In the meantime," said Jonathan, "no peeping."

As Mrs Bird disappeared into the kitchen taking the Advent calendar with her, Paddington hurried to the front door and peered through the letter box to see if by any chance the postman was still doing his rounds, but all he saw instead was a long black car driving slowly past.

It was the longest one he had ever seen. In fact, it was so long he didn't think it was ever going to end, and he went back to the living room to tell Jonathan and Judy.

"It sounds like a stretch limo," said Jonathan, knowledgeably.

"It was a very slow one," said Paddington. "It tried to stop and then it went on again. I think the man driving it was looking for somewhere to park."

"I bet you couldn't see anyone in the back," said Jonathan.

Paddington shook his head. "The windows were all dark."

"That was a stretch limo all right," said Jonathan.

"It must be someone very important," said Judy.

A thought suddenly struck her. She turned to her brother. "You don't think… it isn't someone looking for 'you know who'?"

"Who's that?" asked Paddington.

Judy put a hand to her mouth, but before she had time to answer there was a ring at the front door bell.

"I was right!" she cried. "What are we going to do?"

Taking hold of one of the long curtains at the French windows, Jonathan signalled to Paddington. "Quick! Hide behind here."

Paddington had no idea what the others were talking about, but he could tell by the tone of their voices that it was urgent, and by then his knees were shaking so much he didn't wait to ask.

As soon as Paddington was safely hidden Jonathan turned back to his sister. "I told you we should have done something about making a trap door in the floorboards for him."

Before Judy had time to answer there was a loud sneeze.

"Pardon me!" called Paddington.

"Ssh!" said Judy.

"The curtains are tickling my nose and I can't find my handkerchief," cried Paddington. "I think it must be in one of my duffle coat pockets."

"Too late!" groaned Jonathan, as the sound of voices drew near and the door handle began to turn.

"Guess who's here!" said Mrs Bird.

Scanning the room, her eagle eyes immediately spotted movement behind the curtain. "You'd better come out, Paddington. There's someone to see you."

Both Jonathan and Judy stared at their visitor in amazement. Much to their relief, anything less like a Government Inspector would have been hard to imagine. He was much too short for a start; not a great deal taller than Paddington.

His clothes also had to seen to be believed.

Topped by a wide brimmed straw hat worn squarely on his head, the bottom half, or the little of it that could be seen beneath a multi coloured cloak, was a mixture of styles. The top half appeared to be a black dinner jacket which looked as though it had seen better days, while the khaki trousers, full of bulging pockets, looked more suited to the jungle.

On the other hand, his boots were so highly polished you could have seen your face in them.

When the stranger spoke it was with a mixture of accents, none of which they could immediately place.

"Remember me, *sobrino*?" he called. "Caught up with you at long last."

At the sound of the voice, Paddington emerged

from behind the curtain and hurried across the room, paws outstretched.

"Uncle Pastuzo!" he exclaimed.

"Thank goodness for that!" whispered Judy, taking her brother's hand.

"Who would have thought it?" said Jonathan. "Wonders will never cease."

All of a sudden it felt as though the cloud which had been hanging over their heads had disappeared of its own accord.

Chapter Seven

PADDINGTON'S CHRISTMAS SURPRISE

ENVELOPING PADDINGTON IN his poncho, Uncle Pastuzo gave him a huge hug. "Thought I would never find you, *sobrino*. You ask me how? Is another story. I tell you sometime.

"Been twice round the world since last July."

"You must be dying for a cup of tea," said Mrs Brown.

Along with Mr Brown, she had arrived on the scene rather later than the others, and they were both trying to catch up on events.

Letting go of Paddington, their visitor produced a large watch on the end of a chain. "Gone ten of the clock and I no have breakfast yet!"

"Mercy me!" exclaimed Mrs Bird. "I'll get you something straight away."

Uncle Pastuzo kissed her hand. "*Gracias,* beautiful *señorita,*" he said. "That is music to my ears."

"We have several kinds of cereal…" Mrs Bird went quite pink as she began ticking off various alternatives on her fingers. "There's porridge… kippers… bacon and eggs… sausages… black pudding… kedgeree… fried potato… toast and marmalade…"

"Sounds great to me, *señorita!*" said Uncle Pastuzo, smacking his lips.

The Browns exchanged glances. From the back view of Mrs Bird as she bustled off towards the kitchen it was hard to tell what she was thinking and they feared the worst, but a moment or so later they relaxed when they heard the sound of pots and pans being put to work.

"You know something about travel?" said Uncle Pastuzo. "It makes you hungry."

"However *did* you find us?" asked Mrs Brown.

"It was written in the stars. Heard tell on the grapevine there was a bear living in London. Had a railroad station named after him."

"I think," said Mrs Brown gently, "you will find it was the other way round."

"That is not how it was told to me, *señora*," said Uncle Pastuzo, "so when I reach London I head for the station, and there I see a newspaper headline. Knew at once who they were talking about."

He turned to Paddington. "Began cruising the area. Next thing I know, you are coming out of a shop that has big globe in the window…"

"Oyster Travels," said Paddington.

"Right in one. So what happens? I get out of my limo and shout your name, but by then you had vanished into the crowd."

"I was hoping to take everyone round the world too," said Paddington sadly, "but I only had one Air Mile."

"*Sobrino*, when I get back home you can have all

mine," said Uncle Pastuzo. "By now there should be enough to take you anywhere you wish."

"I don't know anyone who's been round the world once," said Jonathan, "let alone twice."

"Took wrong path in Africa," said Uncle Pastuzo simply. "Turned right instead of left. Went back on myself. Thought everything was beginning to look the same."

"How about your car?" asked Mr Brown. "I wouldn't want it to get towed away. They're rather hot on that kind of thing round here."

"No problem," said Uncle Pastuzo cheerfully. "Fits your front drive like a dream; all ten metres of it! Could have been made to measure."

"I'm sure Paddington's uncle will have it moved when you want to get yours out, Henry," said Mrs Brown, catching the look on her husband's face. "Better that than have it towed away."

"Too true it is!" agreed Uncle Pastuzo. "Rules and regulations! People invent the motor car and make things so you can't live without one. Then others come along and make it impossible to live *with* it! Poppycock!"

"Yes, well…" began Mr Brown. "You try saying that to a traffic warden."

"I did," said Uncle Pastuzo. "One of them tried to give me a ticket when I came out of that Oyster place. Only been in there two minutes."

Producing a giant dagger from under his poncho, he ran his free paw along the length of the blade. "I tell him, you want to watch it, *gringo*!"

"Oh, dear," said Mrs Brown. "I hope you didn't give him our address."

Uncle Pastuzo chuckled. "Me? I was not born yesterday. Gave him your neighbour's number. *Hombre* name of Curry. Heard all about him from Lucy. Seems you two don't get on too well."

"You are in touch with Paddington's Aunt Lucy?" said Mrs Brown, anxious to change the subject.

"First stop when I set out," said Uncle Pastuzo. "There she was, large as life, and twice as happy in the Home for Retired Bears. Knitting away in her rocking chair like there was no tomorrow. Could hardly hear myself think for all the needles clicking: tea cosies, bed socks, scarves… you call that retirement?

"She tell me your address. Only thing is, I remember the number of your house, but forget the name of the road. Not like Darkest Peru. Where I live we only got one. Straight up to the top of the mountain and straight back down again. Got the rest of the address from that Oyster place. That was when I know it was meant."

He turned to Paddington. "Spoke to man in there with bad twitch. Said he knew you well, *sobrino*. Seems like you are not the apple of his eye."

"You will be staying, of course," broke in Mrs Brown. "We can make a room ready while you are having your breakfast."

Uncle Pastuzo glanced out at the garden. "No need," he said, pointing to the summerhouse. "Give me hammer and nail and that will suit me just fine. Like a palace."

"Are you sure?" asked Mrs Brown. "Won't you be cold?"

"You haven't slept outside in the Andes in the middle of winter," said Uncle Pastuzo.

"That's true," admitted Mrs Brown.

"Wake up most mornings with icicles on your

whiskers. Those that have them," he added hastily, not wishing to offend.

"I'd better move the lawn mower," said Mr Brown.

He paused. "Er… forgive my asking, but why do you need a hammer and a nail?"

"Need somewhere to hang this." Uncle Pastuzo reached for his hat. "Home is where you hang it."

With a quick flick he sent his own hat flying across the room. It hovered for a brief moment near the ceiling before landing gently on top of a standard lamp.

"Gosh!" said Jonathan admiringly. "I wish I could do that."

"I teach you," said Uncle Pastuzo. "Is what they call a knack."

"It may be a knack," said Mrs Brown, fearing for her china, "but it might not be so easy with a school cap."

"Meantime," said Uncle Pastuzo, ignoring the interruption, "I give *Señorita* Bird a hand. Make sure she does eggs the way I like. Over easy, sunny side up."

"May I come too?" asked Paddington eagerly.

The Browns looked at each other when they were on their own.

"What do you think he meant when he said 'Home is where you hang your hat'?" asked Mrs Brown. "It sounded a bit permanent to me."

"How long is a piece of string?" said Mr Brown. "I know one thing; if breakfast is anything to go by we'd better get some more supplies in before the shops close for Christmas."

In the end it was Mrs Bird who answered most of their questions. Clearly she couldn't wait to unburden herself when she returned at long last.

"That should keep them quiet for a while," she said, undoing her apron. "Besides, there is a lot of catching up to do. I've left Paddington in charge of the toast and marmalade."

"Tell us the worst," said Mr Brown.

"Well…" Mrs Bird took a deep breath. "Paddington's uncle lives high up in the Andes mountains in an area which is rich in all kinds of precious metals: copper, gold, silver… platinum. Now, who do you think benefits the most?"

"The people who dig for it?" suggested Jonathan.

"Wrong," said Mrs Bird.

"Their employers?" hazarded Judy.

"Wrong again," said Mrs Bird.

"If the car parked in our front drive is anything to go by," said Mr Brown, "Uncle Pastuzo."

"Right," said Mrs Bird. "He has a little store at the top of one of the biggest mines, and when the workers come up at the end of their shift, hot, tired and above all thirsty, he's there ready and waiting with hot dogs and ice-cold drinks.

"They may have spent their time underground looking for precious metals, but Uncle Pastuzo has his own gold mine at the top. In any case, there is nowhere else to spend their earnings.

"Having grown wealthy over the years, he now wants to see a bit of the world while he can. As he says, you can't take it with you."

"He told you all that while you were cooking his breakfast?" said Mrs Brown.

"And a lot more besides," said Mrs Bird. "There's nothing like getting together over a kitchen stove to make people open up."

"Er… while you were chatting, did you get any idea of how long he plans to stay?" asked Mr Brown.

"As far as I'm concerned," said Mrs Bird, "he can make it as long as he likes.

"He has the same big brown eyes as certain others I could name," she added dreamily, "and he's very polite. You can see where Paddington gets it from – along with his Aunt Lucy, of course."

"So what more can you tell us?" asked Mrs Brown.

"Just you wait and see," said Mrs Bird mysteriously. "It's his idea and I wouldn't want to spoil it; especially as it's meant to be a surprise for Paddington."

And there, for the time being, matters rested.

After his mammoth breakfast, Paddington's uncle

went outside to his car and returned carrying a suitcase. Laying it down in the middle of the floor, he opened the lid, pressed a button, and a small folding bed began to erect itself. It was followed by a whirr and a hiss of air as a mattress took shape.

"Bought it in Hong Kong," he said briefly.

"Are you sure you wouldn't like something bigger?" asked Mrs Brown.

Uncle Pastuzo shook his head. "They say that to me when I stay at the Ritz Hotel, in Paris, France. They no like it when I say I prefer my bed to theirs. I tell them – if they no let me use my bed, then I camp out in front of their hotel and hang my washing out to dry. They like that even less."

"It's a wonder they didn't have you arrested," said Mr Brown.

Uncle Pastuzo jingled some coins in a trouser pocket. "Not so as you would notice... *buenas noches.*"

Having said good night, Paddington's uncle opened the French windows, gathered his belongings together and headed towards the summerhouse.

"I'd better move the lawn mower," said Mr Brown.

"Don't forget the hammer and nails," called Mrs Brown.

"It must be nice to be so independent," she continued, closing the door after them. "But it is rather unsettling for the rest of us. I wonder when he wants to be woken?"

"I should leave him be for the time being," said Mrs Bird. "It's best to let sleeping bears lie."

"Perhaps he's hibernating," suggested Jonathan.

"Our geography mistress says bears don't hibernate in the true sense of the word," said Judy. "On the other hand, some of them do go to sleep for months at a time. Perhaps we should ask Paddington?"

"Don't put ideas into that bear's head," warned Mrs Bird. "He has more than enough in there already."

As things turned out, however, they were all wrong about Uncle Pastuzo. The next morning he was up bright and early, and after announcing he 'had matters to deal with', disappeared soon after breakfast and didn't arrive back until late that afternoon.

"If you don't mind my asking," said Mrs Brown, "what do you picture doing for the rest of the day?"

"You mean, what are *we* doing?" said Uncle Pastuzo.

There was a toot from the limousine outside.

"Better hurry," said Uncle Pastuzo. "Otherwise we miss flight."

"Miss the flight?" echoed the Browns.

"That is what they call it," said Uncle Pastuzo, ushering everyone out of the door.

Climbing into the front seat, he settled down alongside the driver and began issuing instructions. But they were lost on the Browns as they entered via the rear doors.

Paddington nearly fell over backwards with surprise when he climbed inside. The last person he expected to see was Mr Gruber, seated in an armchair at the far end.

"It is a small world, Mr Brown," said his friend. "And as I think I once said to you, it gets smaller all the time. I feel very honoured to have been invited."

"It's very James Bond," said Judy, eyeing a bank of television screens.

"Everything except a nuclear warhead," agreed Jonathan.

"I don't think I could live with those curtains," said Mrs Bird, casting an expert eye over the furnishings. "They're far too grand and they don't go with the carpet."

"I hope we don't come across anyone we know," said Mrs Brown, settling herself down in another armchair. "Perhaps we'd better draw them just in case."

"They won't be able to see us," said Jonathan, pointing to the tinted glass, "but if you like…" Running his eyes over a control console in front of them, he pressed a button and the curtains slid together.

"Do *you* know what's happening, Mr Gruber?" asked Paddington.

But Mr Gruber wasn't letting on. "It is something I have always wanted to do, Mr Brown," was all he would say.

Mrs Bird was equally tight-lipped on the subject, and for most of the journey everyone else was kept so busy trying out the various gadgets they hardly noticed where they were going anyway.

When they eventually drew to a halt Jonathan pressed the button again, and as the curtains parted he and Judy joined Paddington at one of the windows.

"Guess what!" said Jonathan.

"It looks like a bicycle wheel to me," said Paddington.

"It's called the London Eye," said Judy.

"We're all going for a ride on it," explained Mr Gruber.

"We're going for a ride on a bicycle wheel!" exclaimed Paddington. "I hope we don't get a puncture!"

"There's no fear of that," said Mr Gruber. "If you take a closer look, you will see there are lots of cabins all round the rim. We shall be travelling in one of those."

"They look as though they are made of glass," said Judy. "They aren't, of course, but it does mean you can look every which way while you are going round."

"And you can stand up and walk around," added Jonathan.

"Thirty-two of them," said Uncle Pastuzo, helping the others disembark from the car. "Each one holds twenty-five passengers. That is nearly 800 people. I book through your friend at the Oyster shop, *sobrino*, and I pay extra so we have a whole one to ourselves. He is so pleased he say any time you want a holiday you go see him."

"Mrs Bird's right," whispered Jonathan. "Bears *do* fall on their feet."

"I fix everything," said Uncle Pastuzo, as a hostess came forward to greet them. "We take what is called the VIP trip. Tee hee!"

"Tee hee?" repeated Mrs Brown.

"Ought to be VIB – Very Important Bears!"

Doubled up with laughter at his own joke, Uncle Pastuzo followed on behind their escort.

The timing was exactly right. As they arrived at the starting point, an empty capsule arrived. The doors slid open, and as they stepped aboard the sun began to disappear behind the Houses of Parliament.

For the first few minutes, as the wheel slowly

revolved and they gathered height, Mr Gruber
pointed out many of the important landmarks still
visible in the gathering dusk to Paddington's uncle:
Big Ben; Buckingham Palace; the Tower of London;
St Paul's Cathedral; the many parks and lakes; and
the British Telecom Tower, silhouetted like a pencil
against the skyline.

Paddington had visited many of them over the
years, but somehow, as London began to unfold
before their eyes, they seemed to take on a different

life, the buildings evolving into tiny scale models of the real thing; the streets peopled by ants and model cars going hither and thither everywhere you looked.

"Is the only way to see the world," said Uncle Pastuzo, pleased at everyone's reaction. "From on high and away from the crowds."

As darkness fell still further, and the capsule gradually rose higher and higher, lights began appearing all over London. Floodlit buildings came into view, and Christmas lights twinkled in the night sky.

They even had a brief glimpse of ice skaters on the far side of the river further round to their right.

There was one slight hiccup almost at the end of its journey, when Uncle Pastuzo called them all together to see what he called "something special", but by the time they had formed themselves into a group the moment had passed.

It had been one long series of magical moments and in the rush to disembark, nobody noticed Uncle Pastuzo disappear for a minute or two. In any case they had grown used to his sudden comings and goings.

On the journey home Paddington joined in the general agreement that it was the best treat they'd had for a very long time.

All the same, Mrs Bird couldn't help noticing that in between whiles both Paddington and his uncle were unusually quiet.

She couldn't help wondering if all the talk about going round the world, and now the trip on the London Eye, had given Paddington itchy paws, but for the time being she kept her thoughts to herself. There was no sense in spoiling everyone else's pleasure.

Uncle Pastuzo dropped Mr Gruber off first.

"You have been a good friend over the years to my *sobrino*," he said, shaking him warmly by the hand. "For that I bless you."

Somehow, as Mr Gruber waved goodbye, it all seemed very final.

The Browns' housekeeper had difficulty in getting to sleep that night, and the result was she woke rather later than usual the next morning. Even so, the house felt strangely quiet.

Slipping into a dressing gown, she was making her way downstairs when she happened to glance out of the landing window and realised Uncle Pastuzo's car was no longer in the driveway.

Her heart missing a beat, she hastened back upstairs to Paddington's room. The duvet was pulled back and there was a hollow in the mattress where he must have lain, but it felt cold to the touch.

On the way down again she found two envelopes lying on the front doormat. One marked '*Señorita Bird*', she put into her apron pocket for later; the other was marked for Mr and Mrs Brown.

Soon the whole household was awake to her calls and everyone came rushing downstairs to see what the excitement was about.

The note to Mr and Mrs Brown was typically short.

"Been there, done that, now is time to go home," read Mr Brown. "So, *amigos*, it is time to say *adiós* and *gracias.*"

"That's nice," he said, once he had got over the initial shock. "Somehow *adiós* sounds better than goodbye; it's not quite so final."

"And *gracias* is so much better than a simple 'thank you'," agreed Mrs Brown.

"The thing is," said Mrs Bird, searching for the right words and hardly able to find the right ones to say what was uppermost in her mind. "Where's Paddington?"

Something in the tone of her voice caused a ripple of apprehension to run through the others.

"He was out in the garden the last time I saw him," said Jonathan. "I think he was doing some early morning digging."

One glance through the dining room window was enough.

Paddington nearly dropped his seaside spade with surprise when he suddenly found himself surrounded by the rest of the family.

"I was looking for some buried treasure," he

announced. "Uncle Pastuzo left me a map he made.

"He doesn't like goodbyes, so he slipped it under my door last night after I went to bed." He held it up for the others to see. "I thought I'd better get up early in case Mr Curry saw me and wanted to know what I was doing."

"X marks the spot where you start," said Jonathan, looking at the roughly-drawn map.

"It says ten paces north," said Judy. "Then five paces east."

"The trouble is," said Paddington. "I'm not sure which is north."

"I'll get my spade," said Mr Brown, by now as excited as the rest of them.

Having followed the instructions, he ended up in the shrubbery. "That's my prize buddleia," he said. "It can't be under that. At least, I hope it isn't."

"It's probably a case of bear's paces," said Mrs Brown. "They're not as long as ours. You'd better let Paddington have a go."

Having first been pointed in the right direction, Paddington set out, while the others counted the steps as he went.

Sure enough, this time the trail ended up in the middle of a flower bed. Mr Brown brushed aside a pile of leaves to reveal a freshly dug patch of earth, and after a few prods with his spade he struck metal.

"Brilliant!" exclaimed Jonathan.

"I don't know about that," said Mr Brown. "It's the box I keep my golf balls in. I hope they're all right."

"Do hurry up, Henry," called Mrs Brown. "Paddington's waiting."

"Why don't you have a go then," said Mr Brown, handing him the spade.

Paddington needed no second bidding and in no time at all he prised the box out of the ground and had the lid open.

The first thing he came across was a canvas bag with his name on the tag. Pulling on the drawstrings he felt inside and discovered it was full of foreign coins.

"Uncle Pastuzo must have collected them while he was travelling round the world," said Jonathan, taking a closer look. "I bet they're worth a bomb!"

Underneath that, carefully wrapped in tissue paper, were seven large glossy photographs of the whole family taken inside the capsule on the London Eye.

"So that's where he disappeared to," said Judy. "I saw a notice on the way in saying if you pose at a certain point a picture is automatically taken, ready to buy when you get off."

"What a very kind thought," said Mrs Brown. "We must have ours framed, Henry. It can have

a place of honour on the mantelpiece."

"I shall put mine by my bed," said Mrs Bird.

"We can take ours with us when we go back to school," added Judy.

"And I shall put mine alongside Aunt Lucy's picture," said Paddington. "I'll give Mr Gruber his tomorrow. I expect he would like it for the shop."

"We shall miss Uncle Pastuzo," said Mrs Brown on the way back to the house.

"He may have been a bit of a whirlwind, but it will seem very quiet without him."

"At least that bear's ends are tied up now," said Mrs Bird. "It's always bothered me."

Having overheard the conversation, as soon as he got indoors Paddington hurried upstairs to his bedroom and examined his reflection carefully in the mirror.

As ever, Mrs Bird was right. He had no idea how or when it had happened, but Uncle Pastuzo must have done a good job. Everything was in its proper place. No matter which way he turned he couldn't see the slightest sign of any knots.

Later on that morning the Browns heard the sound of hammering coming from Paddington's room, but everyone was so pleased by the fact that he was still with them, they pretended not to notice.

"I've been following Aunt Lucy's example," he

announced that evening when they all went up to his room to say good night. "I've been counting my blessings. Except, I wanted to do mine *before* I go to sleep. I have so many I may not have time tomorrow.

"I still have some important shopping to do and I shall need to go to the bank to get all Uncle Pastuzo's coins counted."

"I don't think you will be very popular with the rest of the queue at this time of the year," warned Mr Brown.

"Anyway," said Mrs Brown, "you mustn't go spending the money on us. Your being here is the best present we could possibly have."

"Life just wouldn't be the same without you," added Mrs Bird, amid general agreement.

Paddington pointed to a large nail on the back of his bedroom door. "Uncle Pastuzo taught me one thing," he explained. "Home is where you hang your hat."

Removing his bush hat he tossed it into the air. Much to his surprise it landed back on his head.

"Never mind, Paddington," said Mrs Brown,

amid the laughter that followed. "Practice makes perfect, and from now on you have all the time in the world!"